Mary G Mahony

Marmaduke Denver and Other Stories

Mary G Mahony

Marmaduke Denver and Other Stories

ISBN/EAN: 9783744747509

Printed in Europe, USA, Canada, Australia, Japan

Cover: Foto ©Andreas Hilbeck / pixelio.de

More available books at **www.hansebooks.com**

Marmaduke Denver

AND OTHER STORIES.

BY

MARY G. MAHONY.

SAN FRANCISCO:
WOMEN'S CO-OPERATIVE PRINTING OFFICE,
1887.

The author offers this little collection of stories to her friends with a sincere apology. Firstly, because some of them have been published before in the columns of the newspapers, and secondly, because I am compelled to reproduce them in this shape—by stern necessity. I seek neither name nor fame, but that which is much dearer to me than either, your friendly forbearance and kindly consideration.   M. G. M.

Màrmàduke Denver.

CHAPTER I.

It was the sweet season of buds and blossoms; the fragrant hawthorn breathed a generous largess of perfume through the soft spring air and had already begun to spread a gorgeous carpet of pink and white petals.

In the orchard at Redwood Farm two young people were seated beneath a hoary-looking apple-tree whose gnarled limbs, speckled with grey-white moss gave it a patriarchal eminence among its more youthful companions. From their Titian-like parent sprang vigorous young shoots which triumphantly spread forth a lavish load of satiny blossoms.

Florence Denver was a rosy-cheeked girl of some fifteen summers, plump and healthy and sunburnt, but full of promise of the glorious fruit of beauty which was sure to follow this healthy blossoming. The soft, smooth skin was tinged with a pink hue which seemed to come from the great rose in each cheek; the somewhat large mouth was clear cut and expressive, and the full eyes seemed to have borrowed their color from the shifting hues of the sky— so changeable were they, now light, now dark blue—eyes that would be capable of expressing every emotion.

The boy at her side was so very boyish and awkward, that an observer would never have lingered to bestow a second glance upon him. A man in the chrysalis state—

if we may so call it—is rather an uninteresting creature at best, while the pretty caterpillar which promises the lady butterfly, has usually more attractions of color and contour.

Harold Hereford was so obviously unfinished, so crude from nature's mould, that it would be almost cruel to describe him at this period of his existence, so far was he from having yet "filled the measure of youth." Added to his other disadvantages, he had just developed the uncertain and certainly unmusical squeak which heralds the transition from the voice of boyhood to a manly base. In a word, our readers must take Master Hereford on trust—as we can promise nothing nor prophecy much for such a piece of unleavened earth, and a present estimate of him can only be gathered from his conversation with Florence Denver beneath the apple-tree, and henceforward by watching his career up and down the ladder of life which lay before him.

"And so you are going away to college, Hal," said the girl at his side, "and I sha'n't see you for ever so long," and she gathered the falling blossoms into her lap with a sigh.

" And you will be going to boarding-school," he replied somewhat ruefully, "and you will soon forget all about *me.*"

"Oh, I'll be sure to *miss* you, Harold," she answered, laughing at his lugubrious expression. " You see I have known you such a long time I *can't* forget you."

Her reasons for remembering him did not seem to afford him much comfort, for he looked at her reproachfully, and swallowed an imaginary something. That he was very fond of his playmate ever since the period of mud pies, was a fact of about as much consequence to her as the affection of her favorite dog, but when he produced from its many wrappings of paper, a photograph of himself, and presented to her very solemnly, the girl's eyes filled with tears.

They had known each other since childhood, and he had seemed as necessary a part of her life as her pet dog or most cherished toy, and she felt that she would miss him as such. Childlike they sat there and mapped out their garden of life, as though they alone were the sole and supreme gardeners, and as if there would be no adverse winds to disturb the flowers therein.

A sudden breeze sent down a shower of blossoms upon them, which lodged in her hair, and nestled in the folds of lace upon her bosom. She laughingly bent her head towards the boy that he might pick them out, and while doing so he touched her hair softly and reverently with his lips.

With many good-byes—tender and sorrowful on his side—they parted at the orchard gate, and as the grateful incense of supper floated out upon the evening air, our heroine soon forgot all about love and lovers. Such is extreme youth—in love.

Florence was the eldest daughter of wealthy Farmer Denver, who had leavened a handsome farm out of the primitive prairie, which had, after years of toil, yielded him a generous recompense, and now, at a hale and hearty period of his life, he relegated the responsibility to his two growing sons.

To farmer Denver's mind, the education of boys should consist merely of "readin', 'ritin', and 'rithmetic,"—anything else he deemed superfluous nonsense. "If *I* had gone to college," he was wont to say, "and learned Greek and Latin, and other darned dead langwidges, I would be just one of them good-for-nothing fops as can spend mor'n they can earn." This was his final clincher to any argument on the subject, and the only concession his wife could obtain in this matter was the promise of a tutor who should be sternly cautioned against imparting any of his city nonsense to *his* boys.

Upper-ten-dom was, in William Denver's honest estimation, an artificial structure, whose veneering was often of the thinnest and cheapest kind, and he found much of the grandeur of life in the green glory of his crops and their rich ripeness, wrought by the peaceful plowshare. His great heart, unwarped by conventionalism, was guileless and generous, and knew naught or the shallow artifices of the *effete elegante*. He held the soft-clothed city man in sublime contempt, and eventually fell into the very venial sin of judging them *all* from one standpoint—hence his stubborn antipathy to what he considered superfluous educational and ornamental acquirements.

The pink and white petals of the blossoms had hardly withered among the long grasses in the orchard when the delicate little mistress of the farm sickened, and in one week the patient hands were folded in placid resignation over the dead heart.

Twenty years before Hattie Wilberforce had left her refined home in a great city, and married "Wild Will Denver," her handsome, uneducated country cousin.

She had always been delicate, and her being so seemed to make her all the more dear to the strong, healthy husband, and he had been as tenderly kind to her as if she had been a little child, in all those twenty years.

Her death was a cruel stroke to him, now when fortune had given them the wherewithal to make their declining years still happier. The little wife had never grown old in his eyes, and in his bereavement he thought of her only as the blithe, blue-eyed girl, who had left a higher sphere to share his uncertain lot, for love of him.

They saw but little of him for many days, and when he came again amongst them the brown hair was thickly streaked with white, and the feebleness of old age had suddenly come upon him.

The summer had nearly gone and the leaves had turned to gorgeous hues of crimson and gold before things had resumed their wonted course at the farm.

William Denver had made a solemn promise to the dead wife, as he kissed her white lips for the last time, and he was going to fulfill it as an act of reparation, which was sacredly due. To send her two boys to college had been one of Mrs. Denver's dearest wishes, and it was the only wish in which he had ever decidedly opposed her; but now there was a great uprooting of many old hobbies in the farmer's mind, and a gradual awakening to the consciousness that his whole life had been devoted to the science of money getting, to the exclusion of many higher or nobler objects. Now that his gentle wife had left him, to think and judge alone, he found himself looking at matters with her eyes, and thinking with her thoughts about many things, but particularly of the future of the children.

In due time the two boys, Milton and Duke, were sent to school to a distant city, Florence being sent to a boarding school. Soon after the farmer found himself alone with his grief, which became even more poignant when his little five-year-old girl toddled from her nurse's care to nestle in his arms.

Five years had passed away leaving their meed of joys and sorrows. Gently they had touched the farmer's head, silvering more of the brown hair; lovingly had they dealt with his children—bringing rare beauty to the faces and forms of his girls, and magnificent manliness to his boys. Florence's vacations were seasons of unmeasured delight to the youthful Kataline and her father, and he longed for the time when Florence would be the guiding angel of his house, and in a measure fill the void in his heart.

A perfect picture of beauty was the little Kataline whose sunny, blue eyes and tangled mass of sunny hair made a rare picture of lovely childhood.

And now arose a new necessity in the farmer's household; this "wee lamb" was fast freeing herself from the shackles of the nursery, and the prospect of sending her away to school was so distasteful to the farmer's widowed heart, that he put it off as long as possible and compromised the matter for the present by advertising for a governess who should make her home with them.

A few days later the Lefton *Herald* announced the fact that a "lady teacher would find a comfortable home at Redwood Farm."

Later on during that day the advertisement became an important theme of discussion between two ladies, the occupants of a dingy lodging in the cheapest part of the city of Lefton.

"Do you feel strong enough to undertake it, Madeline?" queried the older of the two ladies in question, with anxious solicitude in her face, and a quavering note of apprehension in her voice. "I'm afraid the doctor will not allow you."

"But it is to the country, mother; going to the country is a very different thing." Her voice was full of a feverish entreaty. "I want the country air; it would do me all the good in the world. The city feels like a prison to me. Pray let me try it, mother."

Madeline Grey's face was almost ghost-like in the intensity and transparency of its pallor. A long and terrible illness had left cruel marks of suffering upon face and form, and the mother's heart sank within her as she gazed upon her stricken child whose life had been blighted in its very prime.

After a long and anxious consultation, it was decided that Madeline should try the position thus offered, in spite of broken health and bruised heart, for the widowed mother was dependent upon this slender reed for sustenance.

She had written to Farmer Denver, and two days after she was seated beside him in the comfortable spring cart which he had almost filled with cushions and coverings to render the thirty miles of rugged country road as comfortable as possible.

William Denver lifted the slight form in his arms, and his touch was almost of a womanly tenderness as he wrapped her around with shawls and rugs, nor did he for one moment stop to consider her apparent want of strength for the duties of her position; in his kindly heart there was only tenderness and solicitude for her comfort.

Madeline Grey was almost silent during the long drive, but her eyes became brighter and a faint tinge of color stole into the pallid cheeks. The pure country air was already doing its work, and a great breath of thankfulness, a wordless prayer welled silently up from the weak heart, as her eyes feasted upon the majestic stretches of mountain and wooded valleys. The air was filled with the glorious incense of clover and ripened hay, making a grand tribute of fruitful nature to its Creator. In all this there was to her an indescribable sense of rest, a very numbness of quiet pleasure that barred out every thought of aught else

save peace, to soul and body, and, if a wish could creep in, it
would be that this driving thus might go on forever, through
such scenes as these, an unending but peaceful and
beautiful day-dream.

The evening shadows were lengthening when they reached
the farm; the great house dog barked sleepily without opening his eyes, and wagging a lazy welcome to his master,
again resumed his slumbers.

For the first time in her life the little Kataline almost
ignored the presence of her father, and clinging to the new
governess held up her mouth to be kissed.

Farm life seemed to agree with the world-worn woman
whose apparent youth contrasted strangely with her shattered health and sad demeanor. There was a settled,
despairing sort of sadness in her dark blue eyes which gave
her a spiritual expression; her cameo-like features were
almost severe in their classical contour, and in repose were
cold and rigid as marble.

William Denver was no connoisseur of character, nor
was he in the least a diviner of the depths and recesses of a
woman's heart. His was not a nature to search beneath
the surface for materials to form his opinions about things
or people. The method of calculation by which he had
arrived at a satisfactory conclusion with regard to Mrs.
Grey must have been a short and simple one. He was
pleased with her, and would as soon think of uprooting a
beautiful flower, which was an unquestioned pleasure to him,
to look for suspected unsightliness at its root, as to probe
or pry into the hidden feelings of people who pleased him,
much less this silent woman who seemed intent only upon
doing her duty.

That Mrs. Grey was a widow, with a mother dependent
upon her for bread was all that he knew, and that much
was sufficient to enlist his warmest sympathy.

Kataline improved rapidly under her tuition, and the girl's attachment to her beautiful governess grew stronger every day.

Little improvements were soon visible through the house, and when Florence came home during her customary vacation, she was at first inclined to shed tears over some of the deposed ornaments—cherished of her childhood—which were replaced by dainty little miracles in needle-work, and exquisite "bits" in pencil which modestly usurped their places.

"Papa has got a governess for sister Kataline," wrote Florence to her brother Duke, "and she looks like the picture of a *saint*, but a very sad one. You could not help thinking that she must have seen something that once frightened her very much, and that she has never forgotten it. I *know* what you will want to do when you see her. You will want to paint her picture, but if you could leave the great *sorrow* out of her eyes, Duke, you would surely fall in love with your picture, like that poor sculptor that fell in love with his beautiful statue. I wish you could see her. Come soon. Love to Milton, from

SISTER FLORENCE "

About the same time Madeline Grey wrote the following to her mother: "I am far happier here than I had ever dared to hope. I seem to think that the things which you and I dread cannot enter here—as well might lightning flash from a clear sky. There is only *one* danger threatening my peace now—it is the home-coming of those young men, which I hope will be deferred a long time. I have seen their pictures, and one is *oh, so like*—but I must not think of this. Your child,

MADELINE."

CHAPTER II.

Duke Denver, whose proper name was Marmaduke, had developed some taste as an artist, while at school, and had been sent to Italy to prosecute his studies. Milton, the oldest, became an enthusiastic student of theology, and so the vocation of the two young men seemed to be decided.

Milton's letters from college were prayerful, pious things, as became an embryo churchman, and Duke's, from Florence, were brimful of life's pleasures, "much of which may be found," he wrote, "in fair Florence, that wonderful treasury of books, pictures and music." Roseate, glowing letters they were, yet boyish and light as the foam of an effervescing draught.

Harold Hereford had become a clever doctor of medicine, and his visits to the farm were numerically like to those of the angels. How matters progressed between him and Florence will be learned in a future chapter.

One magnificent street in Naples, fronts the Bay for miles, and commands many superb views. The shifting, opalistic colors assumed by the waters, the weird and varied lights and shadows born of the voluptuous Neapolitan evenings, and the beautiful as well as grotesque shapes presented by Mount Vesuvius contribute inexhaustible treasures to the poetic and artistic student.

Duke Denver and his companion, a young Frenchman, had somehow managed to secure an attic in one of the houses in this favored locality, which he had likened in letters "to an obscure corner in heaven."

Those magnificent Neapolitan nights—and they are

seldom otherwise—can lull one's senses, wine-like, to a dreamy languor. No one ever desires to stay indoors after sunset. Duke and his brother artist were lounging in the easiest possible attitude, too luxuriously lazy even to talk. Smoking, under the circumstances, was out of the question, and would have required a supreme effort, which, in their pleasant, sublime state of ease, would be closely akin to labor.

The Frenchman was the first ·to break the silence. "Monsieur Denver, what have you done with your little model, that pretty Calabrian child of last year?"

"Oh, gone back to her tribe, I suppose," replied Duke, raising his arms languidly and folding them softly upon his bosom, " or, maybe, found a lover among the enterprising heroes of the Abruzzi."

" A haughty elf she was, too," continued the Frenchman. "I tried to kiss her one day, but she flung herself out of my reach and flashed a look of anger at me that would have done credit to an abbess, though, by my faith, there are dozens of fine dames who would not flaunt Peirre Lacroix—aye dozens."

Duke was not evidently pleased with his friend's remarks for he vouchsafed no further comment, but turned his thoughts to the pretty Sicilian girl of whom he had made a sketch the year before—a waif whose gypsy-like face came sometimes into his dreams. She was one of the people who whined in the usual Neapolitan fashion for alms, but she *sang* for hers, and there was rare melody in her plaintive voice that gained her more money than her poverty could have done.

A pretty face is no rarity among the Sicilian street singers, and artists' models with faces and forms of marvelous beauty were as plenty in that " City of Sanctity,"

as "leaves in Vallembrosa;" even in the highest ranks
can be found fair dames who will graciously *condescend* to
pose for a satisfactory remuneration. Yet above and
beyond all, the modest peasant child retained a higher
place in his thoughts, and her sweet voice like the dreamy
music of an Æolian harp, often floated pleasantly through
his memory.

He had hoped to see her again when he returned to
Florence, and he longed again to hear her voice, which
seemed to harmonize with the soft twilight, blending her
plaint for alms with songs of love, whose import she was
all too young to understand.

There are surely many small byways as well as highways
to the human heart, and it is often reached by strangely
devious paths that are unknown to us and unguarded;
little things often impel us with a strength that is at once
subtle and supreme. Duke did not know which was the
strongest power that made him long so much to visit
Florence again. It might be a chain of many different
links, but he did not know the peasant girl was a link as
strong as any of the others.

Duke Denver's life had been soft-gliding and placid as
a stream without a ripple; he had passed into manhood in
unconscious possession of all the boyish traits and buoyant
hopefulness that belong to youth, and he felt as happy in
his unpretentious *atelier* in Naples, as a man whose
future was assured.

"I'm getting tired of Naples, Pierre," he said at length,
" let us go back to Florence, again."

"You must be surely dreaming, Marmaduke," replied
his friend. "Why, we are not here a month yet, and you
longed so much to come here."

"I like Florence better," replied Duke, illogically, and
he relapsed again into meditation.

" Very well, *mon ami*, you *shall* go, you shall have your whim, if you really mean it. When would you like to go, *mon comrade*? To-morrow?

" Yes, to-morrow," repeated Duke, brightening.

" Hurrah!" responded the cheerful Frenchman. "To-morrow, then, we are *en voyage* again, and *I* shall not unpack *my* valise when I get there until you manage to get a little more backbone into your present weak resolutions."

" *Merci*," said Duke with a languid smile, "you are a cherub, Pierre."

Pierre Lacroix liked the young American, who had an unconscious knack of winning his way into many hearts,— his frank, boyish blue eyes could look the whole world in the face—making good people pause to give him a hearty hand shake, and compelling the other kind to feel ashamed of themselves.

Pierre Lacroix was a veritable Bohemian, good-natured as he was reckless. He had conceived an intense liking for Duke, chiefly because the young American was his opposite in almost everything. Among innumerable other French adjectives he called him " his ballast," "his buoy and anchor," and in pathetic moods " his guiding angel."

He would have gone cheerfully to the end of the world with Duke, and would then, as he expressed it, "hang on by a peg to the outer edge for the pleasure of his company."

The next day saw them *en route* for Florence.

A lovely landscape flitted past the hurrying train like a panorama; the low, grassy hills were dotted daisy-like with little white cottages; the glowing orchards and trim hedges, looking almost artificial in their neat regularity, presented an unrivalled picture of peace and beauty.

They were fortunate enough to find apartments in the old locality and soon found themselves comfortably housed.

Duke had spent a year in Florence and had made many friends there. The day after their arrival invitations poured in upon them from many old acquaintances, but the Princess de Carillo's card was by far the most important in Pierre Lacroix's estimation. The Princess was as popular in Italy as a queen might be in her own dominion; her power was potent in political intrigues, and her wealth almost fabulous. She was a woman without a particle of beauty, and yet whom to know was to love, and whose slightest favor could draw men down upon their knees— aye, almost to death. "A dangerous siren"—so said the world. To-night her gorgeous *salon* in Florence was a veritable fairyland of light, and music, and flowers.

Our young artists arrived late but were fortunate enough to get a glimpse of the princess who was leaning upon the arm of an Austrian Ambassador, whose very evident admiration seemed to weary her. A smile lighted up her face when she recognized the two young artists.

"*Mon enfants*, how good you are;" (the princess was barely twenty and invariably assumed a maternal air towards the young men of her acquaintance) "how very good of you to come and see a tired old woman. Seeing you back again," she continued, "is so pleasant; it is like mending a broken chain, after finding two of the lost links again." As she said this she dismissed his Austrian greatness with a grace and sweetness that were inimitable, and then motioning the two young men to a divan seated herself between them.

Duke, as might be expected, was not much of a courtier; his tongue could form no such honied speeches as her ears were accustomed to hear, and yet, strange enough, in this very defect lay his greatest charm in her eyes. The unsophisticated American was a novelty to her, and there was positive refreshment in his out-spoken, unstudied thoughts and unconventional manner. A French woman's life, it is said, revolves upon the pivot of matrimony, adulation and flattery being two of the most important levers in the matrimonial machinery. Up to a certain period Hortense de Carillo's life had revolved like most others of her sex, and then she was married, at a tender age, to a man who was older than her father, totally unable to discriminate in a matter about which she was scarcely consulted, and too young to realize what love meant.

The gorgeous vista pictured to her by a marriage with a wealthy old man, completely satisfied the ambition of her untutored school-girl heart, the release from a stern parental rule being the most sublime sort of emancipation in a French girl's mind. This was what she felt, standing in the fairy portals of marriage, when the voice of the youthful heart was easily stilled, when love was stifled even before its birth, and then she was whirled into the vortex of a soulless, gilded life, in which heart and conscience held no share.

Hortense de Carillo had reeled through the maze but a short time when the stifled heart-cry became a passionate plaint. Her husband, a blasé man of the world, had never loved her, and his blunted sin-gorged sensibilities were not a whit disturbed by the knowledge that she found no pleasure in his society. They saw but little of each other, and she was free to amuse herself after her own fashion, provided, '' she made no scenes,'' nor eloped with any one.

Surrounded with all that could apparently gratify a woman's senses—wealth and adoration—the princess was

restless and unhappy. Satin and diamonds cover, alas!
how often, a starving heart, and the flashing light of jewels
can never warm its dreary chambers.

Without the sun no plant can be healthy, no fruit can
ripen, no flower can gain color or perfume, nor can the
human heart flourish without its meed of sunshine—which
is love. Denied of this it will ever crave in its wordless
language, and mutely spread out its golden tendrils eager
to twine themselves around some loved object. Alas! for
the poor heart whose hunger is unappeased; whose still, small
voice is unheeded; whose tendrils are flung back to shrink
and wither, hiding forever their dead leaves in the empty
heart.

Duke had been telling the princess about his pretty
model whom he had found in Florence. "*Mon Dieu,*"
murmured the princess naively, "how I wish I were a
peasant girl, with soft black eyes and a sweet voice."

She sighed naturally enough as she said this, and bent
her brown eyes for a moment upon the young American.

"And you would console yourself with a lurking hope of
some King Cophetua's making his debut at the proper
time," laughed Pierre Lacroix, as he twisted the ends of
his mustache.

"You must let me see that picture sometime, Monsieur
Denver. I am quite interested in your gypsy queen," said
the princess lightly, "and I hope for your sake that she
may be the lost heiress of someone who is somebody; and
she has a sweet voice, too," she continued. "If you find
her again be sure and bring her to me. And now,
Monsieur," she said, rising, her billowy lace foaming
around her, "I must leave you ; but pray, don't forget
my request, nay, my command (this with mock sternness) to
bring the child to me," and with a charming smile, from
which a thousand sweet regrets shown, she left them.

Hortense de Carillo's face was not one to attract any notice, if one did not happen to know her. The small face was plain almost to homeliness, and the quiet brown eyes were nearly expressionless, but when she smiled—and in that lay all her glory—her lips and all her features assumed the most bewitching expression, and seemed to be illuminated by a strangely beautiful light. "She should be always smiling," said many of her admirers. It was her greatest power—a force that brought lovers by the hundreds, who forgot their allegiance elsewhere while basking in the entrancing atmosphere which this woman diffused around her.

It is difficult to analyze the heart, to arraign its thousands of varying emotions before the tribunal of reason. A year had passed since she had first met Duke Denver, with his boyish, beardless face, and artless tongue, and now the shackles, golden though they were, that bound her, felt cold and tight, and cruel as death, and the brave religious heart that had hitherto been as a giant bulwark against dishonor, was, alas, even now reaching out its weary tendrils towards him.

Duke had passed into manhood without losing any of his boyish fancies. Before he was seventeen he had formed an ideal for himself, one that he had conceived by the pure light of an innocent heart, and because of this the wiles and witcheries of society women had but little power over him, and he emerged from many a gorgeous labyrinth with his beloved ideal graven more deeply upon his honest heart.

"Let us go, Pierre, I am tired of the salon," said Duke, after the princess had left them.

"Certainly, *mon ami*," replied the other, smiling; "it is only a dreary desert when *she* goes away. You are

right" he added, "she will not come near us again to-night.
What an angel she is; but her *visites* resemble *theirs* a little
too much. *Allons mon enfant.*"

In truth, Duke was not thinking of the princess just
then. He longed to get back to his rooms, and sit upon
the pleasant veranda where he had first heard the sweet
voice of the peasant girl whose face had often come to him
in dreams.

This soft-eyed child of the Calabrias, a beggar in the
streets of Florence, had a face which an empress might
stop to wonder at, and when she sang her simple chant for
alms, there were few indeed who did not pause to look and
listen.

Trustfully and innocently she had followed Duke to his
studio one day, coming again and again, without a thought
of danger, and she often sang for him when her voice
seemed a part of the twilight and the evening odors of the
flowers, while her great eyes, that Fra Angelico would have
loved to paint, tried to find him up there in the darkness
upon the veranda.

After he had gone to Naples she had come there night
after night, not knowing that he had gone, and when at
last she had realized that he was no longer there, she sang
from house to house through the whole city, caring but
little for the coins that were flung to her, heedless alike of
the coarse jokes and flatteries which were still more lavish,
hoping to find him, until at last, weary and hopeless, she
went, no one knew whither, perhaps to other cities to look
for him, for she had already made of her simple heart a
pedestal, whereon she had placed him, to be worshipped in
silent and sorrowing reverence.

The rich blood of Sicily becomes warmed to love's tem-
perature at a tender age, and the kindly behaviour of the

young American, free from raillery or coarseness, had reached the childish heart—unlocking it all too soon—with its hidden treasures of love.

Night after night Duke sat and listened on the veranda, hoping to hear her again, and by day he often peered anxiously among the groups of peasants on the streets, but he never found her.

" *She* will find *you* some day, be assured," the princess had said to him one evening, "and then you shall make me a present of her, and some day," she added thoughtfully, "you shall hear a charming singing bird whom you shall want to capture for yourself."

" What a romantic web the princess can weave around a prosy old fellow like you, Duke," laughed Pierre Lacroix, looking at Duke in mock admiration.

It was Duke's habit on such occasions to allow his friend full scope for the witty and polite retorts upon which Pierre prided himself not a little, and although the princess laughed good-naturedly at them, she never failed to look expectantly to Duke for some reply.

" If I remember aright," said Duke, slowly, "the nymph or siren who knitted or crochetted those mythical materials was called "Daphne."

" Yes," suggested Pierre, " something that begins with a D, I think."

" Oh, yes," chimed in the princess gayly, "and the materials she used were ' rays of sunshine,' and ' threads of moonbeams fringed with dewdrops ' and other airy nothings."

" Oh, but *madame la princess* would need some stronger stuff to enclose *that* young Hercules," said Pierre, pointing to Duke. "The finer web might do for *me*," he added, plaintively. " I'm slight and tender——," " "And innocent as a child," interrupted Duke, with a genuine American grin.

"Oh, golden warp and silver woof," sang the princess softly, as if her voice was away in the distance, and a sudden shade of sadness came into her face. In all that gorgeous maze of music and mirth, and the perfume of flowers, her heart was beating heavily and becoming more than ever conscious of its terrible void.

She arose to accept the arm of a white-haired old general, who claimed her for the waltz which was just then commencing.

Duke followed her with his eyes, thinking the while how pleasant it was to be near her, and listen to the voice which had such lulling power.

There was an indescribable something about the woman which pleased one in an easy, passionless way—something more akin to the nature of music or sunshine, or the pleasure that one derives from the presence and perfume of flowers, inspiring the reverence that one might feel for a thing of beauty and goodness.

CHAPTER III.

About this time the fact began to dawn upon Duke's lazy imagination that he was becoming a hopeless idler, purposeless and indifferent. He roused himself just enough to wonder at it, but did not inquire very closely into the matter—it is not easy to grasp at will—or define the oft-times intangible causes of our failings for analysis. Duke was a little puzzled about it, but at length comfortably concluded that it was nothing worse than the inevitable *ennui* that one is sure to succumb to in the lazy, luxurious indolence of an Italian climate. But he was exceedingly conscientious, and deeming himself too partial a tribunal to be arraigned before, complained to Pierre of the growing inanity which was besetting him of late·

Your case is just this, *mon chere enfant,*" replied Pierre tenderly, as if he dreaded to hurt some sore spot on Duke's mental person. " You are very young. *Mon Dieu !* horribly young. An American is always an *enfant* in his own land, but in Paris, Florence—Gods, he is a *babe.* Then your appetite is not regulated for these climates; you take over much *wine* at your repast, *mon frere.*"

" Wine," echoed Duke, staring in astonishment, " you know I never drink, Pierre."

" Oh, I mean your banquets of pleasure, your feasts of reason, etc.; your sun-bathing in *madame's* eyelight, the wine of her smiles. You are a glutton, *mon chere,* a drunkard, a-a—but you don't know it, you don't know yourself, you are a *babe,* you——"

" Oh, stop, for heaven's sake!" cried Duke, throwing up his hands as if to defend himself from blows. " You are on the wrong track, as they say in America, and that eloquent peroration of yours is a tissue of nonsense."

" I will prescribe for you, I will save you," cried his friend, tragically. " You shall be more moderate; you shall do violence to your weakness; you shall live; henceforth, thou shalt labor with thine hands."

"Yes," sighed Duke, flinging the end of a cigar away, " but you talk nonsense, Pierre; I am not in love with anyone, least of all with another man's wife."

" *Of course not*," replied his friend calmly, with a grin that would have made his fortune as Mephistopheles; " men seldom get mad in a minute, or drunk in a moment. You are not quite poisoned yet; some potions work slowly, but they *kill* all the more surely."

" Nothing so common as that hallucination of yours, dear boy," Duke retorted; "*you* are the one who is in love, and think, naturally enough, that everyone must needs see with *your eyes*."

" Time will tell," responded Pierre, prophetically; " this air is *my* native element, old man, and you *can't* drown a duck in water."

" Well, granting that all you say is true, what would you prescribe for the sad case?" inquired Duke. " What shall I do that I may be saved?"

" Keep away from the *salon* of the princess for a month and paint something—me, for instance; it will take some bitumen, but the exercise is good—try it."

" All right," replied Duke, tilting his chair back and closing his eyes; " 'tis a cruel punishment, but it is some satisfaction to know that you must suffer some of it."

For the first time in his life Duke found himself meditating seriously. In this shower of nonsense which his friend had jocosely launched upon him, he seemed to feel a slender shaft which pricked him with a keen sting. The influence of his simple country home was still strong upon him; as yet there had been nothing in his life to awaken strong emotions. He was a religious man, too, and a willing prisoner in the chains with which the Catholic Church guards the passions of its followers. That anyone should suspect him of being in love with a woman who belonged to another was inexpressibly shocking to him, when put into words. Even if he *had* been unconsciously drifting into a liking for the society of the princess, these words of his friend rudely dispelled any self-illusive shading there might have been, exposing a naked and hideous fact, and proved him by the light of his own conscience, a criminal, and he began to feel like a man who had just been dragged from the brink of a dangerous precipice. Under the influence of these feelings, he resolved to keep away from the *salon* of the princess, and at least disabuse the mind of his friend of this monstrous idea.

More than a month had passed and Duke had kept his resolution bravely. His abstinence, as Pierre termed it, was not as easy a task as he had imagined, though they both tried to "make merry" over it, and Pierre grimly intimated at times, "that it was hard to live without the light of the sun." There was more truth in his wit than either of them dreamed of.

It had been an unusually warm day in Florence, and people gladly welcomed the evening with its drowsy hum of softly dying noises, which lessened gradually until snatches of laughter and occasional bursts of music alone broke the stillness. A little later the theatres commenced to pour forth their throngs, whose merry voices and laughter sounded wonderfully distinct through the still air of the city.

Our two young artists had been to the theatre and were
elbowing their way out through a dense crowd, which began to scatter as they approached the Piazza de la Signora.
Here a good many people paused to listen to a serenade
which was going on before one of the houses.   Duke
Denver stood for a moment to listen, and then started
quickly forward as he recognized a well-known voice.
Pierre tried to hold him back.   "Wait 'til the song is
over," he said, in a low voice; "then we will find her."

The crowd listened breathlessly to the wildly-beautiful
music that welled up from those untutored peasant
throats:

> In Venice, when the sinking sun
> In blushing beauty seeks the West,
> When purple shadows softly blend
> Their colors with the deep blue sea,
> A sound comes stealing near and near,
> Until it rests within my heart,
> And of its pulses seems a part--
>   The singing of the Gondolier.
>
> When tender flowers droop and swoon
> Beneath the perfumed pall of night,
> And trembling trees show leaflets white,
> All silvered by the pale moonlight;
> Now faintly near, now sweetly near,
> Now faint and far, now deep and clear,
> A lingering memory ever dear—
>   The music of the Gondolier.

Many carriages had crashed past the little group of
listeners and had rumbled softly away in the distance.
As the song ended the people turned to disperse, and no
one seemed to notice the nearness of a vehicle, which was
close upon them, until the fiery eyes of a pair of runaway
horses flashed upon them, and in a moment more they had
dashed through the crowd, tramping a path over prostrate
forms.   It was all so sudden, that no one saw the driver
crouching in helpless terror upon the box, holding on
with both hands and clutching one side of a broken rein,

and inside a woman's face white and rigid with fear. All was now confusion and screams, where a moment before was only music and peace. Duke had been borne down in an attempt to grasp the horses, and was mercilessly crushed beneath their feet. A square further the maddened brutes crashed blindly against an archway, one falling dead, and so entangling the other as to render it helpless. The driver, almost paralyzed with fright, now clambered feebly to the ground and thrust his head into the still un-injured carriage, with the ghastly expectation of finding his mistress a corpse, but the Princess de Carillo—for it was she—had recovered from her terror and stepped now firmly on to the street. Through the whole hideous crush she had never lost consciousness; she had seen the horses beating down the little crowd in the Piazza, and knew that some of then must have been injured or killed, and in spite of the lateness of the hour and the remonstrances of the still trembling coachman, she walked quickly back to the scene of the accident. The rough pebbles almost cut through the thin satin shoes, and there was but little pro-tection in the flimsy lace shawl around her head, but she was a generous and kindly-hearted woman and did not con-sider herself when people needed help.

"Come, Leon, and be quick," she said almost angrily to the coachman ; "I'm not afraid." When they reached the place they found that five people had been hurt, and were being carried to their homes by friends. Pierre had gone in search of a carriage. At a little distance from the rest she saw a group bending over a prostrate form. There was an ominous stillness among them. As the princess approached them one of the women rose to her feet; an-other, a mere girl, sat upon the ground, and held the sufferer's head on her lap. The princess stood over them for a moment, and then sank weakly upon her knees, as she recognized the deathly white face of Duke Denver. She forgot the people who were looking on, and the girl who sat supporting his head, and who now glanced jealously up at her, and in a moment the white jewelled arms, bare and cold, were around him, drawing him towards her. The young girl arose and fell back a pace or two, and stood gazing, with tightly folded hands, at the woman in white, who looked so like a beautiful apparition.

"Quick, Leon, go get a carriage. I know him. I will take him to his home. Come to me to-morrow, if you need help. I am the Princess de Carillo."

Her voice sounded harshly, as if the utterance of words pained her, and she bent again over the still, insensible form, holding him as tenderly as one might hold a child. They brought him to her house, where the doctors were soon in attendance. Pierre was almost distracted with grief and forgot his own bruises. He remained with Duke all night, and mourned his young friend as already dead.

Duke did not become conscious until the next day, and then he lay helpless and speechless, the graceful young form, quite paralyzed. No murmur of pain escaped him, and the princess could only tell by the look in his eyes, when she came into the room, that he knew her. She could notice a faint flush on the pallid face, as she bent over him with sad beseeching eyes. It was unutterable agony to her to see him lying thus, and she would have shed her heart's blood, if it would have given him life enough to speak one word to her.

The doctors were puzzled about the case, and would not give much hope. "A severe injury to the spine had affected the brain. It was dangerous—very dangerous," they said, "but his magnificent physique might surmount it." Every voice in the house had been hushed to the softest whisper. Three days had passed since the accident, and there was still no change in Duke's condition. The princess was almost in despair, and now looked for the death which would surely take some of *her* life with it.

One evening when the crimson glow of the sunset stole into the sick chamber, a broad beam fell upon the sick man's face, and surrounded his head like a halo. The princess sat near him, her head drooping upon her hands. She looked up suddenly and saw the glory of light upon his face, and making a golden aureole of his fair hair. The wide blue eyes were looking straight at her, full of melting pity, as if he fain would speak and comfort her. She thought with a thrill of fear that this must be death— holy and awful to her. For a moment she sank upon her knees, awed and reverent in its presence, and then, something that had become infinitely stronger than holy fear, arose in her, and she drew the unresisting head close to her and kissed the still dumb lips again and again. Then she laid him back softly upon the pillow and went away, covering her face with her hands, as if to keep that last look of his in her eyes forever, and walked unsteadily to the room where the doctor was still waiting.

But the "grim white steed" took his departure at last, and a change for the better set in; even the doctors were surprised. The rigidity of his limbs began to relax and he gained strength rapidly; his own voice was the first to break the long silence in his chamber, and her *name* was the first word that he uttered.

They sent for her and she came quickly, but paused in the doorway so that she might hear his voice and compose herself. She waited in the darkness of the doorway until the doctors should leave the room by the door leading to

the main hall, "for no one must see the Princess de
Carillo weeping over the young American stranger."

She could hear his voice, weak and querulous as that of
a child, asking to see her, but she could not stir then to
save her life. She dared not go in yet, but not a word,
not a sigh of his escaped her. The doctors went away
at last and then she went softly in; she had composed herself, although her face bore ineffaceable traces of acute
anguish.

His eyes lighted up joyously as she came towards him;
there was a questioning, too, in their blue depths that he
could never put into words—it was soul speaking to soul,
in which no words could avail.

"You have been suffering for me," he said softly, as
she put her hand into his, "and it nearly killed me
to——" but she put her hand gently over his mouth and
he said no more. Great tears of thankfulness were in her
eyes and dropped upon his face as he held her hand in
happy silence.

The doctors soon returned and she became her own
superb self again. Pierre Lacroix was with the doctors
and his joy was like that of a schoolboy, a mixture of
laughter and tears.

In his boyish, affectionate way, Duke had liked the
princess, and had actually felt very young and insignificant
in her eyes. To submit to her kindly patronage seemed
quite natural to his simple, glowing nature, and matters
might have gone on thus for a lifetime without awakening any other sentiments in his heart; but such friendships
are often dangerously blind as well as beautiful.

The princess left the room with a sweet smile upon her
face and walked slowly to her own chamber, where her
pride and fortitude deserted her, or rather, were flung

aside, and a wretched woman grovelled upon the floor because of the love which was a shame.

Some souls grow stronger as the body weakens—it may be that the spirit detaches itself from its earthly shell—gathering its scattered strength unto itself, and stands alone in its own purity.

So also does the spirit sometimes weaken as its earthly rind withers and falls away. Duke's soul and body sank together and were now craving, child-like in their weakness, for the comfort that his soul would, in its strength, have rejected. With returned health he might beat this weakness back from heart and brain, though quelling the surging tide of a young heart is an Herculean task and might be more than he could accomplish.

Just now he did not trouble himself about the right or wrong of it; he had no strength for any mental exertion, but lay quietly, a strange, happy languor upon him which he did not care to disturb.

The princess came to see him but seldom now, and he understood her reasons; she only came when the doctors were there. The memory of that kiss, given, as she thought, in his dumb and dying moments, seemed to linger upon his lips, and was freshened by the loving memory in which he held it. There was in it much of boyish longing for her woman's kindly touch, but its fatal sweetness gathered strength with returning health, eating its way to his very soul, and fanning the dormant fire in his nature to an unquenchable flame.

He sprang quickly into health and strength, now, and as he did so, the visits of the princess ceased entirely, and he could have wished that he might lie there maimed and helpless all his life.

We are taught to buffet what is antagonistic to body and

soul; and most of us are educated and strengthened by religion to combat the sins which we know by name, but there are innumerable untrained emotions, intangible weaknesses, which are our most fatal foes, because they are born of the human heart, every day and hour of our lives, and for which we have no laws, no rules, forever troubling us with questions which we know not how to answer, and menacing us with danger which we are almost powerless to ward away.

Duke Denver's boyhood had passed quickly out of sight forever. The placidity of the calm, religious-tinted soul in him, which had been like a clear lake in the sunshine, was now stirred to its deepest depths, bringing much that was earthly in it to the surface, and a swift and troubled current into his life.

A few days after Duke had left the house of the princess, her maid came to her with a puzzled face.

" Madame, there is a person, a girl, who has been here very often, to enquire about the health of M. Denver; some creature, no doubt, who should be sent away."

" What does she look like, Marie?" questioned the princess, with a thoughtful air. " Perhaps," she added hastily, " she comes from some of the people who were hurt by my carriage. Did she wish to see me? Let her be brought to me."

"Yes, madame, if the porter has not sent her away; he has grown tired of her coming so often."

" Go quick, Marie," said the princess, angrily, " and bring her back."

In a few minutes the maid returned, followed by the Sicilian peasant, the girl whom Duke Denver had told her about, and the princess recognized the girl who had been holding his head upon her lap when he lay for dead.

The princess gazed at her in silence, as if her mind were occupied with something else, and then begging Marie to leave her, she motioned to the girl to come nearer.

" I know what you would ask, child—for M. Denver, is it not ?"

"Excellenza, yes, pray tell me that he lives, that he will not die," replied the girl with an imploring gesture, " He has been kind, ah! so kind to me;" here she quailed and clasped her hands beseechingly.

For a moment a wild, unreasoning anger filled the bosom of the princess against this wretched child, who could and might love him without sin or shame, but only for a moment, and then the woman's better nature asserted itself, and when she spoke again her voice had a broken, pitiful tone. " Yes, girl, he is well. He has been kind to you?" Her voice grew softer now. " Ah, who would not be," she murmured more to herself, as she noticed the slim, graceful outlines of the form, which promised a magnificent maturity. The thin, clinging garments upon her were old and faded, but there was in every wreath and fold an unconscious beauty.

The faint dusk of red in her olive cheeks deepened as she stood there, embarrassed and irresolute. " She is not a bold girl," thought the princess, " Oh, far, far from it. *Mon Dieu*," she murmured, " but it nearly cost her her life to come here, and yet she would walk upon burning brass to get news of him. *Sapristi*, what a face she has. But you are standing, my child," she said; " I had not noticed. I am sorry. Pray sit down."

The princess now relapsed into deep thought. " And I am the one who has destroyed him," she said to herself, "and I am, alas! powerless to save him, to help him. *Mon Dieu*," she sighed almost aloud, " *my* help would only

complete his ruin. Presently she turned to the girl:
" You can sing, I believe."

"Excellenza, yes; in my poor way," the girl replied.

" Will you sing for me now?" the princess asked, with
one of her sweet smiles.

The young peasant looked at the gorgeous surroundings
for a troubled moment, and then her eyes rested upon the
face of the princess in a mute appeal, as if she thought
her singing would be incongruous in the presence of so
much magnificence, but the reassuring smile of the princess, who quite understood her, gave her some courage,
and she commenced to sing. The sweet mouth quivered
at first and the words came tremblingly, and then the
sound of her own voice seemed to render her oblivious of
her surroundings, and it grew and swelled in strength and
sweetness, the stream-like flow of the melody scarcely
rippled by a word, so soft is the accent of Sicily; even the
patois of the peasant is so softly lipped as to be scarcely
distinguishable in song. Not till her song was finished,
so wrapped was she in her own exquisite music, did the
girl's cheeks redden, but now the rich blood diffused her
face until it fairly burned, and she seemed sadly conscious
of having done a very bold act.

" Charming," murmured the princess, though somewhat
absently. Already she had commenced to plan a scheme
in which this young girl might play an important part, and
her brain had become so busy that she had not paid much
attention to the girl's singing, but she had heard enough to
know that she possessed the germ of a superb voice, and
with such a face and form, too, she thought, could be
easily improved into a magnificent woman. The princess was thoroughly herself now; all the womanly kindness
and generosity of her nature were aroused, and became

powerful factors in the plans which her busy brain was now weaving. She dismissed the young girl with a request that she would come to her on the morrow with her parents.

The next day Veronica, for such was her name, arrived with her parents, who were easily persuaded to allow the girl to be sent to school, where the princess assured them she would be taught all the arts of music and singing, and, moreover, promised to help them, as they were very poor, and Veronica had been their chief support.

The princess attended to all the arrangements for sending the girl to school with a feverish sort of joy which had in it a linking pain. Her noble efforts in this matter were wrung from the keenest self-sacrifice, but, when all had been completed, and she had kissed the girl farewell, a flood swept through her soul, calming, consoling, and purifying, because of this act of God-inspired justice and atonement, the conception of which was worthy of a goddess.

But there was something more to be done—she must see Duke Denver again, though she knew it would wring her heart to its very roots. Her note to him was without name or date, and ran thus: "I ought not to send for you, and cannot blame you if you refuse to come. I want to ask your forgiveness. I am trying, with God's help, to undo the wrong which I have unintentionally done." This was the hardest part of the task which she had set herself to do, but she would shrink from nothing now.

3

Pierre Lacroix was too kindly hearted to plume himself upon the fulfillment of his jocose prophecy, but was now cursing himself unmercifully for what he considered was his fault in allowing his young friend to fall into trouble. He had regarded Duke as a mere boy, whose love, he thought, would be only a youthful effervescence which would quickly boil over, and vanish like a bubble. He loved Duke as a brother, and loved him well, after his own fashion. Wild, *blase*, and godless, he had scarcely an atom of feeling for men of his own mould; though he played, drank and caroused with them all his life, not one of them found room in his thoughts an hour later.

To the young American, whose boyhood seemed to be ever freshly springing within him, whose rare honesty and purity were ever mildly reproachful to him, Pierre had given all the affection of which his reckless nature was capable.

To other men he could freely boast of his excesses, but he could no more tell of such things to Duke than he could to a refined woman. He was terribly pained because the unruffled calm of the young man's life, which was hitherto like the placid bosom of a clear lake, was now tempest-tossed to its deepest depths. The thing which he had dimly feared had actually occurred, and Duke, for the first time in his life, had sought a wretched oblivion in the treacherous wine-cup.

The Frenchman had seen intemperance in all its stages, unmoved, but a pain which had in it the bitterness of death, had wrung his heart when he came home one evening, and saw the fair boyish face flushed and feverish, a reckless light in the blue eyes, and the handsome form flung in utter helplessness upon a lounge.

He had seen wrecks of men who were once of the "purple and fine linen" order, he knew of such things every day in Paris, but they seemed as nothing beside this—this destruction of what was to him almost an idol.

The princess had secretly dreaded this also. She feared for him because he was so young, and, to her mind, without a man's endurance of disappointment.

She waited, day after day, for news of him, but no answer came.

In sheer agony she said to herself, "If he does not come, I will go to him," as visions of his despair, of possible self-destruction haunted her; but it came at last—a little note, written in an unsteady hand, and ran:

"I would come to you, oh! so quickly, but not in the spirit you would wish. God has given you the grace which he has denied to me. If I look upon your face again, I will be something that you would abhor. Pray for me, that I may be enabled to take your image out of my heart. It is so filled with you that I dare not ask God for help."

The note dropped at her feet, and she clasped her head between her hands. She knew now that he still loved her hopelessly—that he was suffering, and that she could do nothing to help him.

"He *cannot* come to me," she moaned, "and he is right. I should not have asked him; but how shall I know that he is safe?" There was only one thing now for her to do, though it would be a bitter humiliation—it was to send for his friend, Pierre Lacroix, to take him into her confidence. But that meant nothing less than a total loss of dignity—of disgrace to name and race, and she could face death a thousand times more willingly than even the shadow of dishonor. There was a bitter struggle in her heart now, between humility and pride, but her love was truly that in which "self was lost and slain." Body and brain must now suffer for the guilt of the heart—if guilt it was. The struggle was fierce and brief, and out of it came a woman with throbbing brain, and white, bloodless lips, but with a heart purged and purified by self-humiliation.

The very quintessence of love is assuredly a total annihilation of selfishness. True love can only exist in the light and sunshine of another's joy—happy only in the reflection of another's happiness. There was none of the "barren bulb of selfishness" in this woman's love; the pleading heart-plaint was no longer for herself, the love flower which had grown unbidden in her sunless path, now lay crushed and fruitless.

Such a woman as Hortense de Carillo could be great in her deepest humility. To succor a man who could be naught to her on earth, and make him happy, was now the dominant desire of her life; to write to Pierre Lacroix was a task easy enough now, and she sent for him.

He came quickly and brought news which chilled her blood. He was very ill, he said, and if she wished to come he would not recognize her. She went back with Pierre Lacroix in her carriage, humbly and passively, listening meekly to all that he said.

Duke lay in a hot fever, his young body scorching in pain. He never knew who bent over him for many days, waiting humbly and reverently upon him, feeling neither shame nor cowardice—the task was to her now one of holiness.

Again the fingers of death were clutching at his heart, striving with cruel kindness to still forever its hopeless pain.

His fevered brain was busy with images thousands of miles away. "How cool your hand is, Florence. Oh! don't take it way. How changed you are, my sister. I had always thought your eyes were blue, but they look black now, and your hair is streaked with grey." He thought himself a boy again, playing with her the old games of childhood. "How strong you must be, Floy, to drag me out of that river where I might have drowned,'' he murmured with a shudder. Anon his face would brighten as he fancied himself once more among his native fields and forests and the surroundings of his home, which had constituted a wide and happy world to him. The present seemed wholly eclipsed by the memories of his boyhood, and the woman who listened in anguish to his fevered ravings could not help thinking that it would be a rare mercy if he died thus—his mind filled only with the unsullied memories of childhood. At times his mind came back in a hopeless jumble, to the present, dragging the tired brain into labyrinthian realms of confusion; this, she could only read in his troubled face, but his tongue never uttered a syllable of the present.

A change for the better came at last, and he came slowly back from the doors of death.

At the first assurance of the doctors that the danger was past, the princess went away, leaving her secret, if such he might deem it, in the possession of Pierre Lacroix.

The doctors had ordered Duke to return to his native land as soon as he was able to travel, and a week later saw him ready for the journey.

When a woman tries to rise above the earthly grossness of her pride, the journey upward is slow and painful, the steps thereof, cruel and cutting, but they soon grow smooth by suffering, plainer and more accessible by the clear light of a pure motive, and the final award is the grace which can only be purchased with pain.

On the journey home Duke was too helpless, both mentally and bodily, to think much about anything. He felt like a person out of whose hands the business of life had been taken forever, and was dimly conscious of having been drifting aimlessly, giving himself up to a sort of blind-folded happiness, and following helplessly a beautiful mirage which had now faded quite away, leaving him in troubled darkness. He had also a pitiful sense of paralyzed energies, as a man who had become suddenly old and feeble. These were some of the glimmerings which his brain weakly grasped as he journeyed homewards.

There was a sort of mental comfort in the winding and rushing of the train, the moving without effort, being carried along through sunny scenes of field and farm, of smooth-flowing rivers and majestic mountains, now near, now distant—all being bathed in a soft haze. To many weary souls there would have been something of mockery in all this peace and beauty, but Duke's was not a mind to envelop itself in " sheets of bitterness," however gloomy it might be; it was somewhat of an open-work fabric, which could not entirely resist the sunlight, and could even absorb some of its rays. He was not keenly miserable now; no doubt, he might realize that with returned health. Betimes, too, he felt like a man floating upon a boundless sea, a white ship appearing ever and anon in the distance, the soft lulling waters seeming to carry him farther away from it. In his dreamy, half-convalescent state, this strange sea became, in his imagination, the cold stream of conscience, pure and limpid, in which he saw his own life clearly mirrored. He could see his errors reflected, not in great crimson stains, but in softened color and outline, as objects seen through depths of water. It was a gentle, silent stream, which seemed to flow through the inner channels of his soul, purifying and healing, and ever bearing him away from the snow-white ship, which still remained in sight, and though it had never beckoned him on, he knew that it contained for him a delirious and deadly happiness.

He reached home in the mellow autumn when the woods were assuming gorgeous hues of gold and crimson. Soft winds moaned with a lonely cadence among the whispering leaves, as if mourning the departed summer. The few remaining flowers were about to breathe their last perfumed sigh before the rude hand of winter should lay them with their sister leaves.

William Denver drove to the railroad depot in the next town to meet his favorite son, who had left home five years before, a strong, lusty youth, with life enough in his young body to last a century, and now the shocked father scarcely recognized him, so pale and thin he looked. They had known from his letters that he "had not been well," but were totally unprepared for this. The poor old man made a great effort to hide his grieved surprise, and replaced it with a feeling of secret indignation—born of the old objections—which still lay dormant in him, against all processes of refinement and improvement. Hot, angry tears rushed to his eyes until he could hardly see. This, he thought, was the result of tasting the poisoned fruit of fashionable life. He would a thousand times rather have seen him a healthy, sunburnt farmer—those small, blue-veined hands of his, rough and horny from toil.

The father eyed his son furtively as they drove home, and did not dare to look broadly at him, fearing that he should

see the anguish which he knew must be in his face.   Duke
was glad to see his old home again.   There are few cases,
indeed, of mental trouble, that are not alleviated in some
degree by a visit to the scenes of youth, that bright and
pure period of our lives athwart whose undimmed light the
world seldom casts a shadow.

Florence was waiting for them at the gate—grown to a
tall and beautiful womanhood.   When she saw Duke's pale
face the smile left hers, and the cheery words of welcome
died upon her lips; she could only open her arms wide and
bring his head down to her lips in silence.

A few weeks at home improved him rapidly.   Florence
had lovingly constituted herself his nurse and he gladly
relinguished himself to her care.

" Do you know that you have grown to be a beautiful
woman, Floy?" he said to her one day as she sat upon a
low chair by the lounge where he lay.   " But you have
not told me anything of Harold Hereford. When is he
coming ? "

"Oh, he only makes a flying visit once in a while," she
replied with a slight blush; "he has been busy since his
appointment to the asylum."

" When have you seen him last, Floy ? "

" About a month ago, Mr. Curiosity."

" Love him as much as ever, Floy ? " he continued.

" Oh! Duke, what a merciless inquisitor you are; how
many more questions must I answer ? " she exclaimed,
putting her hand over his mouth.   " *Now I* am going to
ask *you* some."

" Oh, as many as you please," he said, laughing; " but
you don't happen to remember any apple blossom period
in *my* existence, and," he continued, with a twinkle of
mischief in his eyes, "and you did not care a pin about
him, did you, Floy ? "

" And *you* were mean enough to watch us from the summer-house," she retaliated, with the air of a person who had suffered from an unpardonable injury in the past.

" Milton was a party, in fact, the ringleader in that outrage; but he *was* an awful gawk, Floy, and one could not help making fun of him; but don't be angry, Floy," he laughed, seeing that she made no answer, " I won't tease you any more," and he drew her head down to him and kissed her.

" But where is your Mrs. Grey? " he resumed, after a pause. " I have been home a week and have not seen her yet. Where does she keep herself ? "

" She has gone home, Duke, for a week or two; she went a few days before you came. Her mother has been ill. We feel quite lonely without her. Oh! Duke," she continued, " she *is* lovely, and you must be careful or you will lose your heart to her. Oh! won't it be *my* turn then," she continued, laughing. " I will have you both right under my watchful eye, and will have a chance to pay you back."

" You are welcome, Floy," replied her brother, " when you *do* get the chance. I think," he added, " you said something to me in one of your letters about her hair being grey."

" Yes," replied Florence; " the contrast between her grey hair and young face is very strange, and her eyes are simply divine," she added enthusiastically.

" I have been dreaming," said Duke, somewhat absently, " a weakness peculiar to idle artists, I believe, of a woman with just such eyes as you have described, but I'm afraid I have already found my realization in a peasant girl of Sicily, who once honored me with a sitting. I found her begging in the streets of Florence, whining in the usual

continental fashion, but *her* voice had a pathetic sort of
melody in it; but your description of Mrs. Grey also suggests something of a mystery. I'm curious to ee her. By
the way, Floy, is she aware of *my* existence ? "

"Oh! yes," replied Florence; "she knows that I have
two brothers, and she has seen your pictures."

" Which of the pictures did she consider the better-look-
ing ? " asked Duke, with feigned anxiety.

"I don't know, Mr. Vanity; we may find that out after
she sees you both, and besides," she continued archly,
" there is more pleasure in making those kind of discov-
eries yourself."

The winter was pleasant at the farm-house, and Duke
felt it doing him good. Though rapidly acquiring health
and a certain peace at heart, he felt very much like a
dark silhouette against the bright background of home
happiness, and knew that he could be no contributor to it.

Moreover, he had lately essayed the lugubrious task of
self-analyzation, " a complete going over," as he grimly
phrased it to himself, and having found himself sadly
" wanting in the balance," he manfully endeavored to
impose upon himself the Herculean labor of self-punish-
ment.

To dilute with coldness the warm liquid in youth's
veins, to calm and stem its impetuous current, were tasks
as easy, indeed, as the turning backward of a mighty
river; to deaden the dull pain in his heart, to live
stupidly and forget—forget—would be about as easily ac-
complished as the rest, but he conscientiously undertook
the task, with what results shall be seen anon.

About this time he went to spend a few days with an
old school-fellow in the next town, and had not expected
to be back until the day before Christmas, but he came

sooner than he had intended. He arrived when it was dusk and entered the house unnoticed, going straight to the low-ceilinged room which they had dubbed the library; he threw himself into an easy chair, and, without intending it, was soon fast asleep. He was awakened by someone touching the keys of the piano very softly. Whoever it was only the treble notes were sounded, and an air picked out with one hand. He listened quietly, thinking that it must be Florence or Kataline. The air was unknown to him, an old-fashioned, weird thing that reminded him of Sicily and Veronica.

Duke had become somewhat lazy of late, and luxurious of habits. He liked to sit still and have his senses pleased, and the simple old tune in the dark accorded wonderfully well with his feelings just then. To disturb him at the time would have been a species of cruelty.

But it was neither Florence nor Kataline, for they both came in together soon after and spoke to her.

It must be Mrs. Grey, he thought, as she answered them out of the darkness.

"We are so glad to have you back again, dear," said Florence, "and Duke will be back in a day or two," chimed in Kataline, joyously.

By this time Duke began to feel like an eavesdropper, and rose to his feet, feeling uncertain what to do next. It was quite dark and they could not see him; the old boyish bashfulness and irresolution were strong upon him, and he finally beat an inglorious retreat through the door leading to the garden, and no one knew of his return until he presented himself at breakfast the next morning.

A slight figure in black standing by the fire-place turned to him as he greeted his sisters, and Florence said, "Mrs. Grey, my brother, Duke."

The first thing that impressed him was the peculiarity of her hand shake. Unlike most women she did not allow her hand to lay passively; there was a perceptible clasp, a kind of clinging retention, as though she had entertained kindly opinions of you, and was determined to make friends with you, "taking you by storm." Duke thought there was something in it also that brought to his mind the old Eastern custom of securing protection from an enemy by snatching a morsel of bread and salt.

She regarded him steadily for a moment, as if trying to find something that she had feared, and then she turned away with a relieved expression.

What a tell-tale face, Duke thought, as he warmed his hands before the fire; she is plainly trying to hide something—something that is not her fault either—what a pity. I have read and dreamed of violet eyes, but have never seen the real kind until now. In his poetical imagination she was like a beautiful flower with a cruel weight upon it.

"Duke," said his sister about a month after, "I want you to do something."

"You *do*, Floy," he answered, laughing; "pray what might the great *something* be?"

"It is a pleasant pastime, I promise you *that*," she replied decidedly.

"I'm ready sister mine; unfold your plans."

"Duke," she said in a solemn voice, that forbade all further joking, "I want you to marry Mrs. Grey."

"A decidedly novel request, Madamoiselle Management," laughed her brother, with genuine amusement in his face; "but would it make any difference to your favor if *she* refused *me*?"

"Never mind about that, Duke," she answered seriously,

"that will all come right in time; I have my heart set on it, and you must not disappoint me, Duke."

"Of course you are joking, Floy," replied her brother, trying to look serious, "but really among my numerous sins I have not yet developed the fungus one of vanity, and if I were the best fellow in the world I don't think she would care about me. Now there is Milton, for instance; don't you think he would be a more suitable parti?" As Duke said this he really for the moment stepped down from the comical standpoint from which he had been regarding Florence's novel proposition, and began to take a more serious view of the situation wherein Milton and Mrs. Grey might be the principal figures.

"But you know Milton *can't* marry," said Florence. "He is to enter the church, and you will be the only one left," she added, with an air of desolation.

"Florence," said her brother, "you might as well expect me to fall in love with a picture or a statue, and I fear I lack the necessary ambition to make a modern Pygmalion of myself. She is very interesting to me from an artistic point of view, but *love* is a warm feeling that needs something more of flesh and blood to rest upon."

"Oh, you artists are all conceited," replied Florence, impatiently, "and you have queer ideas about women."

"To convince you that I am not conceited, Floy," replied her brother, "I will say just this much: you must know, *mon enfant*," he commenced oratorically, "that no one can consistently admire man, woman, or thing for beauty or goodness, unless they possess, in some degree, the attributes of that which they admire; ergo, I am not vain or presumptious enough to admire things that are infinitely superior to me, not having the shadow of a corresponding quality to warrant me in aspiring."

"Oh nonsense!" replied the sister, giving the fire a judicious poke. "You are good enough for any woman and every one likes you —and—— "

"I don't deserve it, Floy, it's a mistake; no one will ever fall in love with me—but tell me something of the *modus operandi*, Floy. *I'm* a mere novice in affairs *de la cœur; you* have been eminently successful, and could give me some 'points.'"

"Oh, Duke, you are a humbug. Have you never made love to anyone, never seen a woman that you could love ?"

"Leading questions, every one of 'em," he answered, running his fingers through his hair; "but women are all so different, you know, and what might win one would scare another away. Now Milton is the sort of fellow *she* would take a fancy to, I'll bet you, Floy," he continued with a sudden inspiration of prophecy; "but wait till *he* comes."

At this junction Florence was called away, and Duke was left to his meditations. Mrs. Grey was a sort of study to him. She was different from any woman he had ever known, and, unlike any that his imagination could have conceived; there was nothing *decided* about her, but an unobtrusive suggestiveness of all that was sweet and good, leaving you space, as it were, to magnify each quality a thousand fold. She seemed to breathe a pure atmosphere around her, and one could no more harbor an unholy thought in her presence than he would within the sacred precincts of a sanctuary. She was a woman that he could revere with all his soul, but she could never touch his heart.

"I wish Milton would come," he thought, as he flung the end of a cigar in the fire. "There is a leaf folded down in some chapter of her life, and it strikes me that he will be the one to find out what it contains." Duke liked to weave romances for other people, and he was now busily manufacturing a web for his brother and Mrs. Grey.

Milton came home one snowy day in the new year when the snow shone like diamond dust in the winter sunshine. He was a good-looking fellow, very thoughtful, and grave and cold.

Florence adored him in silence, actually seeming to feel that he was composed of holier clay than herself, and Duke was thoroughly disappointed in his brother and not a little disgusted to find that because a man studied for the church he should become a solemn and silent misanthrope. In his inmost heart he thought it a shame that all the natural life and spirits should be knocked out of, or worse still, repressed in, a man because he " takes care of other people's souls.". For a couple of weeks he had Milton steadily under his mental microscope; he was much given to studying people lately. "But it won't *last*," he said aloud to himself one day, as he had concluded a brown study convincing the present mental mould of his brother.

> "Oft what seems a trifle,
> A trifle, a mere nothing by itself—
> In some nice situation turns the scale
> Of fate, and rules the most important actions."

A month had elapsed since Milton came home and there was a troubled look in Florence's face and a shapeless fear in her heart. She longed to take Duke into her confidence, but being something of a philosopher, she shrank from giving actual shape and substance to her fears by telling them.

The first time that Milton and Mrs. Grey met she had watched them attentively, some indefinable impulse urging her to do so, and she had seen Mrs. Grey's face blanch to an awful whiteness, and she also noticed that she had avoided him since then. These things worried her, but she kept her peace.

"What do you think of Mrs. Grey, Milton?" she said to him one day, in a tone of apparent unconcern. Milton lifted his quiet brown eyes from the book which he was reading and looked at her in an enquiring manner.

"What do I think of Mrs. Grey?" he repeated. "Well, Floy, I have not thought much about her, that is," he added, "I have not tried to form any opinion of her, if that is what you mean."

"But you can't help seeing that she is very nice, Milton," persisted his sister, gaining courage from his evident indifference about the matter.

"I don't think I ever had a very good look at the lady, yet," said Milton, laying down his book, "but if you say that she is nice, Floy, I am certain that she must be so— but she usually sits in a corner and seems to envelop herself in shadows when I am around. Wait," he continued, laughing, "'til I see her in broad daylight and then I will tell you what I think of her *face*, at least, if I may be pardoned for presuming to criticise her."

Florence had, woman-like, developed some match-making abilities, and considered herself a necessary lever in that subtle machinery, as far as the interests of her brother Duke were concerned. That Milton should renounce the church and marry, was to her mind little less than a heinous crime, and the two dearest wishes of her heart just now were to see Milton enter the church, and Duke to marry Mrs. Grey.

Though Madeline Grey was exceedingly reticent about her affairs, and never spoke of her past life, Florence shared her father's opinions, and had perfect confidence in her. If there was some secret trouble in her life, and

Florence could not help thinking sometimes that there was,
she respected her silence on the subject, and never considered it as a fault, but loved her all the more because of
the shadow which seemed to follow her.

For the present she made up her mind that there was nothing to fear concerning Milton, and she knew that Mrs. Grey
was not a woman to fall in love with any one in a hurry.

So little interested was Milton in the study of Mrs.
Grey that he soon forgot his compact with Florence, and
would possibly have given her one of his absent-minded opinions the next time she asked him for it.   But one day a slight
circumstance aroused a lazy sort of curiosity in him concerning her.   He had not noticed that she had been avoiding him, and he came upon her unexpectedly one day in the
parlor.   She was looking very intently at an old picture of
his upon the mantel-piece, and did not hear him approach
until he was near her, and when she turned her face to him
it was deathly pale and her lips were bloodless.   She
made a movement as if she would leave the room, and he
saw that she staggered.   He came quickly to her side,
saying quietly: " You are not well this morning, Mrs. Grey,
allow me to help you."   He led her to a chair, and left
her, saying, "I will bring some water."

She would fain have risen and fled before he returned,
but something held her there, as if some powerful will had
laid its fiat upon her, and she was compelled by it to sit
there and await the return of this man, from whom she
might well flee to the uttermost ends of the earth, and yet
he had never given her a thought, much less an evil one.

She raised her eyes to his as he handed her the glass of
water.   There seemed to be an unspoken command that
she should do so, and it was the very thing which she
wished to avoid.

4

Milton was a stolid, undemonstrative fellow, and it required something almost miraculous to awaken any strong emotion in him. Just now he felt only a species of curiosity, mingled with some pity for Mrs. Grey, and a very man-like inclination to hand her over to Florence's care. He did not think for a moment that the mediocre likeness of himself upon the mantel had anything to do with her faintness. After that day he saw but little of her, and the fact began to dawn upon him, dimly at first, that she was avoiding him, and he became more convinced of it from the fact that when he stayed a few days in the next town—which he did frequently of late—he could learn from their conversation, when he returned, that she had been more among them during his absence. This, coupled with other little things, which became more apparent each day, had the effect of finally exciting his curiosity, and creating a desire to know more about her. It was a decidedly new sensation to find a woman even faintly mirrored in the dull lethargic depths of his mind.

The grim study of theology is well calculated to congeal the tender sap in a man's heart, creating a sort of frozen surface whereon a woman's face could hardly ever make an impression.

He liked to look at Mrs. Grey, because away from her his memory retained no definite image, and this, he thought, was partly due to the fact that she never yet had looked directly at him long enough to allow him to study her face. When they sat around the fire in the winter twilight, she usually placed herself where only an indistinct outline of her face and form were visible to him, and then it was exceedingly pleasant to listen to her voice with its low, sad cadence, when her face was half hidden by the flickering fire shadows. Her conversation, too, was singularly free from hackneyed phrases, and was invariably tempered with mild, but firm, individual opinions, given with a soft decision that made willing converts of her listeners.

They all began to notice that Milton made himself more sociable lately, "owing, no doubt," observed Duke, "to the cheerful comfort of the fire which brought them together more."

Duke generally accompanied a remark of this kind with the most innocent expression, which only those who knew him well could interpret into mild sarcasm. Milton *was* more sociable now and did not pay as much attention to his studies as heretofore, but yet he did not seem to bestow much attention upon Mrs. Grey. If he was studying her he was certainly doing it in about as cold and deliberate a fashion as he would with the very driest, theological treatise. He had, however, made up his mind about two things: that she was very beautiful and that she had some secret sorrow which had been unjustly laid upon her shoulders. Thinking about her, even in this very dispassionate way, made his conscience feel a reprehensive twinge, but he quieted it by the reflection that it was certainly part of his prospective calling to consider the cases of those who were evidently weighted down with sorrow, and he honestly began to think that he might in time win her confidence, and as a minister of God try to lift the burden which seemed to be crushing her life out.

About a month after her meeting with Milton in the parlor, Madeline Grey wrote the following letter to her mother:

"As a blight mars the verdure and healthfulness of a tree or flower, sapping and searing it to the very roots, so again has this misery come upon me. Oh, not come

yet, dearest, but it is close upon me, so near, so threatening that I have not strength enough to flee from it.
My cure is so evenly mixed with poison that I long, yet
fear, to drink of it.   Oh, why does not God take away this
dread burden from me!   It is a thousand times more
cruel than death.   They are *all* here now, happy, and I
feel like a serpent among them, dangerous to them and
to myself.   There is *one* here who looks like *him*.   Advise
your poor   Madeline."

It was several days before the answer came, blurred with
tears, an unhappy mother's heartache between every line,
yet blended with a last feeble hope.

"My poor child:—If it is as you fear it would be best to
come home at once.   You must trust more and more in
Him who is greatest in his mercy.   Your returned health
will be a strong shield.   Use every effort to divest your
mind of the past; in *this* lies your greatest safety.   I know
God will help you, and give you back your lost happiness.
Come, if you think it best.   I am praying for you.
                                        Mother."

CHAPTER V.

Three years had passed away. At this time Pierre Lacroix was speeding from a distant part of Normandy towards Paris; he had been hastily summond to a death-bed there, and would not have lost a moment for the worth of France. He took little heed now of the vine-clad banks of the Seine, and was utterly blind to the blue mountains of Normandy, whose graceful outlines were barely distinguishable from the summer sky—oblivious to everything save the shocking knowledge that the Princess de Carillo was dying.

Arrived at the Rue Saint Domineque, he went quickly through the gorgeously pillared halls where masses of dying flowers shed their petals at his feet. A softly trickling fountain alone broke the silence. Grandeur impresses one but sadly when the presence of death chills its brightness and breathes an icy mist upon all that was wont to glitter. He had been often in that house before; its magnificence had pleased his artist eyes, its music and flowers had charmed him, but to-day every one of its beauties palled upon him; the mirrors flashing from the walls seemed to mock at him, the marble pillars were like so many gravestones, the whole house a gorgeous, gloomy vault. A minute more and he was ushered into the chamber of death. The attendant left him noiselessly and he found himself gazing upon a sad and strange scene. Between the opening of the heavy bed-curtains he caught a glimpse of a pallid face; it seemed to him like the shadowy face one sees in a dream, and he saw it as if through a mist. The faculty of hearing is wonderfully acute in the dying. He had not been announced, yet she knew that he was there, and she motioned to him to come nearer, with the same old smile upon her poor white face, as if there was nothing wrong.

There are some warm natures among human-kind that are fond and foolish and brave enough to be angry even with death, wanting to drive it forth, to fight it away.

Pierre Lacroix had no religion. God was a mere myth to him. He could not pray even for the greatest boon that prayer could bring, but, instead, his loving heart, his strong arm, his life, were ready to be offered—to be interposed between death and those whom he loved. There was chivalry enough in his heart now to fight a thousand deaths, could it be done, to give this woman life. He approached the bedside, but could not utter a word. Our deeper emotions seldom reach the lips. With the keen instinct of those about to die, she understood much of what he felt. She held out a thin, transparent hand to him, and then, like the last flush of a dying sunset, a faint tinge of color replaced the deadly whiteness of her face. She had waited for the last moments before she sent for him, and for what? The aching outcries of the heart are seldom heard; many of them we dare not utter; sometimes they can be read, but are not always written. Pierre Lacroix could easily read a pitiful want in the dying face, and he knew also that she would ask for nothing. He had heard of her illness, but never dreamed that it had come to this. He knew now that she had waited until the last before she sent for him, and impotently cursed himself for not finding out the true state of affairs before it was too late.

Question and answer passed between them without words, a despairing query in the dying eyes and an answer in the stricken face of the man whose heart bled for her.

He raised the wan hand to his lips and bowed his head low over it; there was little need of words here. In her faithful heart she said, "*It is better not;*" in his, he said, "*It is too late, now.*"

She felt his hot tears dropping upon her hand, as it lay in his amid a long silence. She felt, and he knew it, as a modest being who sends for a physician and must needs show wounds which they fain would hide. She had sent for him and yet could not show him the miserable heart-sore which had never healed.

"It is better, Monsieur Lacroix," she said at length, as if resuming a conversation which had occurred only in both their thoughts, "and it is not so awful to die after all, when it comes near. I am glad that this——"

"Die!" he interrupted almost fiercely, "you must not speak like that, madame." He could think of the possibility of her death, although certain of its nearness, yet to hear it from her own lips, was like receiving a stab into a fresh wound. It was terrible to him to hear her speak of death with the light and brightness of youth in her eyes. She seemed to grow more beautiful as the embrace of death closed around her.

> "Ah! ne'er was beauty's dawn so bright,
>   So touching, as that form's decay
> Which, like the altar's trembling light,
>   In holy lustre fades away."

The doctors had diagnosed the case, and had dignified it with some unpronounceable name, but it had simplified the matter soon enough by turning into rapid consumption "of the heart," thought the poor patient with a smile, which was an equal mixture of grief and gladness.

She lay back upon the pillows now, completely exhausted. This last scene, which she had dreaded and longed for, was too much for her waning strength. A faint pressure

of his hand as he gently released hers, told him that she
was still conscious; then a faint whisper—he had to bend
low to hear it: " You will write to him and say good-bye
for me. It will be all over soon. I—want—him—to—
be—happy; come—again—to-morrow; you—are—very—
good."

Pierre Lacroix left the room softly, and the house very
quickly. " It is impossible, I fear," he said to himself, as
if following out some train of thought, as soon as he reached
the street, " but I will try. Great God! what an idiot I
have been; I should have been here long ago. True, she
would never see him living, but it would make her death
less bitter. I think she would see him now." The poor
fellow began to hope wildly, and against all reason, that
Duke Denver could get to Paris before she died; aye,
Pierre Lacroix, a scoffer at prayers and miracles, prayed
now for the first time in his life, that she might live until
Duke came, and believed that his presence would, miracle-
like, save her from death. He rushed to his rooms and
searched with feverish haste for Duke's address, and then
hurried to the nearest telegraph office. "Come quickly,"
he said, "the princess is dying; lose not a moment."

He had dared to do this and felt relieved when it was
done. He knew that Duke would come, and *he* would
dare to bring him to her; he would save her in spite of
herself.

He knew also that Hortense de Carillo's lips would
never say, "Let him look upon my dead face," but that
her heart cried out for it.

After Pierre had left the chamber of the princess, the
door of an ante-chamber opened and a young girl entered.
She came into the room with such a softly gliding movement that she might have been taken for a beautiful appari-

tion. She was dressed in a splendid robe of gold colored satin, half covered with rich lace. Her neck and shoulders were quite bare, save for a necklace of natural rosebuds and leaves, whose dewy loveliness seemed fitting ornament for the fair young flesh which they seemed to caress. The rich dress looked more suitable for an older person, and the sweet, child-like face, seeming to rise from a circlet of flowers, was a unique contrast to the dress, and the massive jeweled bracelets, which were much too heavy for the small wrists. She was a very lovely, but strangely inconsistent picture in that chamber of death.

"You are already dressed, my love," murmured the princess, as the girl approached her. "How beautiful you look! Come nearer," she added, and she took the girl's hand and put it to her lips. To have this girl, so full of youth and life near her, seemed to imbue the dying woman with new vitality. Her eyes brightened, and her face became animated, and she seemed to feed her sinking spirit from the magnificent largess of the girl's youth and health.

"You sing to-night before the Empress, Veronica. How I wish I were there to see your triumph! I know it will surely be one. The Empress herself will fall in love with my singing bird," she continued, smiling, "you are so lovely and so good—so good. But you have an hour yet, *mon cher*," she said looking at her watch, "and it would be charming to hear the rest of your history. I think we stopped last night at the beginning of your love affair."

"Dear madame, you dignify it by too grand a name," replied the girl, blushing. "Poor girls do not dare to *love* great people. They only worship at a distance, and

Monsieur was only kind and charitable to me; oh, so good
and kind!" she exclaimed, clasping her hands together.
"It made me *good*. I could think of nothing evil. I could
do nothing evil while I thought of his kind face and his
gentle voice, and—and—I was thinking of him *all* the
time, and I still think of him," she added, after a short
pause, as she covered her face with her hands.

"And he went away?" said the princess, softly.

"And he went away," echoed the girl, her bosom heav-
ing now, and her eyes filling with tears, "and I searched
and sang for him from door to door, and then from city to
city, but he never heard me until—until—" here the small
mouth quivered and she hung down her head, as if the
bearing of her long concealed secret was a shame.

"Until he was hurt," said the princess, "and went
home to America. But you shall see him again, Veronica.
Monsieur Denver will come back again *to you*."

The princess lay back upon the pillows now, her eyes
closed and her lips moved as if in prayer. It must have
been communion with God in the unreadable language of
the soul, intelligible only to *Him*. There was an indescribable radiance in her eyes, when she turned them
again upon Veronica—a light such as a star might have
lent to them. She drew the girl's head down to her and,
kissed the fresh, young lips lingeringly. "You *shall* see
him again, sweet," she murmured. "When you do, tell
him that *I loved you*."

That night while the plaudits of a vast multitude, were
ringing in the theatre Francaise, and the young prima donna
was almost smothered beneath the flowers, which literally
rained upon her, the spirit of Hortense de Carillo was
winging its way from earth.

*   *   *   *   *   *

A hopeless and desperate man walked the streets of Paris as the bright spring sun lighted up the roofs and shining spires of that great city. His heart almost as dead and cold as that of the loved one who lay beneath a marble slab in Pere-la-Chaise. Marmaduke Denver had arrived in Paris the day after the princess had been buried. In his quiet American home he had been growing calmly content. His dormant love had hedged him round like a delicate lattice work, through which he had learned to gaze out upon the world in subdued sorrow. The memory of this hopeless love became a hallowed thing, which was as pure and holy as it was hopeless, but the shock of her death had completely shattered this beautiful illusion, which might have been a holy seam in the fabric of his life. He felt now as if the light of the world had gone out forever, for him, and a pitiful numbness had grasped every faculty. There was only one thing clearly before his mind, and that was, that which he thought he had conquered was only sleeping, and had now arisen with renewed strength so assert itself.

He knew now *why she died*—he knew also, too late, why she would not send for him, and the knowledge was terrible.

To love and lose is, indeed, like unto standing upon heaven's threshold, and drinking for a space of its intoxicating pleasures. To be driven away, and remain forever thirsting for that which is irrevocably lost, is but a faint comparison to the sufferings of those who have truly loved and lost.

Oh, love! thou art a powerful factor for good or evil; searing and blighting like a curse, or blessing us with the greatest earthly happiness, dispersing the darkest shadows, or bringing darkness to the brightest places. Thou art a

priceless jewel in the humblest home, and miraculous as
the wand of a magician, and without thee we are as the
unripened fruit and colorless flowers.

Pierre Lacroix's great heart throbbed in unison with the
grief of his young friend, and he wished that he had not
summoned him at what was indeed the " eleventh hour."
He knew that Duke's love for the princess, as the wife of
another man, would ever be a thing apart from selfishness
or sin—that it became purer and holier with time.   He
understood also, as well as Duke himself, that he had
manfully resolved never to look upon her face again, and
would be content if he only knew that she had put him
out of her heart; but Pierre felt that all this was changed,
now, that his telegram had revealed a thousand things
that he had better never have known, and that Duke
would now regard himself as the destroyer of her life and
happiness.

People had paid but little attention to the young girl who
had bent over the dead princess, and clung so passionately
to the lifeless lips.   There was no society reserve to stem
the natural outflow of the singing girl's love and grief, and
Veronica Venella nearly broke her young heart when they
bore away her kindly benefactress from her sight forever.

Looking upon her grave in the gorgeous cemetery of
Pere-la-Chaise was a poor sort of comfort, but it was the
only spot in the world in which Duke had any interest now,
and Paris, with all its brightness, was a hideous desert to
him.   He came to the cemetery every evening, when the
frost was crisping the grass and early flowers.   He was
later than usual one evening, and it was quite dark when
he reached there.   He could distinguish a woman bending
over the grave in an attitude of prayer, and he saw that she
held some flowers which she touched with her lips, and

then laid them tenderly and reverently upon the grave.
Her rich dress was trailing upon the damp earth, and when
she stooped to gather it up, the shawl fell back from her
head, and the moonlight showed a face that Duke thought
he had seen before. She had now seen and recognized
him, and drew back tremblingly, as though about to fall,
but he came quickly to her side, saying in a gentle, reassuring voice, "Veronica?"

"Yes," she replied simply, "I am Veronica; and you—
you are Monsieur Denver?"

He took her face between his hands, and raised it to
the moonlight, gazing into it long and earnestly.

"You knew *her*, Veronica?" he said, very softly.

"Yes, oh, yes, Monsieur," she replied sadly, "and she
bade me tell you that *she loved me.*"

He still held her face between his hands, as if she had
been a child, and there were great tears in his eyes as he
bent lower and reverently kissed the unresisting mouth,
and then, taking her by the hand, he led her to her home.

Hortense de Carillo would fain have lived to complete
the work which she had so nobly conceived, but even now
above her grave the unseen chain was forming, which
would link those two young lives together. That this girl
should be the saving angel who would lift Duke's heart out
of the withered weeds in which it lay buried, had been the
cherished ambition of her heart.

Veronica lived with her mother in a pleasant home
which the generosity of the princess had provided for
them. She was now the youthful star of an opera company which was about to travel, and they were to sing
only one night more in Paris.

"You will come to hear me sing," she said one evening to Duke and Pierre. "We are going away." The

girl longed that Duke should hear her and she felt that
his presence would be dearer to her than that of ten thous-
and people.

Going to a theatre *now* would have been ghastly even
in thought to Duke and his friend, but it was "to hear
Veronica," and they would go. It was the last night of
opera in Paris, aye, and they little thought that it was the
last amusement that the gay city should see for a long
time, or that the red cloud of war which was now gathering
over unhappy France would drench the nation in blood
in a few weeks.

They went to hear the young *debutante* sing. They were
both very fond of music—Pierre passionately so. They
found that the young Sicilian star was "all the rage."
People were wondering—as they do when rich volumes of
music well up from the tiny bosom of a bird—where the
wondrous wealth of voice came from, when they beheld
the small, frail form of the singer.

Veronica's voice had in it a rare quality; its strongest
notes were tremulous and sympathetic. It was a voice
"with tears in it" that seemed to reach the heart like a
balm, soothing and healing and awakening feelings that
lay deeply buried. It was like a magic key opening the
locked chambers of the heart and bringing forth goodness
that might have lain forever hidden.

Veronica came upon the stage nervously and looked
straight at the audience, as if she would fain find her
friends' faces. The poor child felt that the theatre would
be empty if they were not there. The small, child-like
form in its old-fashioned dress, the complete absence of
theatrical "make-up," and her perfectly natural manner,
brought her closely to the hearts of the people, and they
greeted her night after night with a generous meed of honest love in their applause.

When the opera was over they went to the green room where her mother was waiting for her, and took them home. Duke felt refreshed and pleased. This evening had, indeed, been like an oasis in his desert, and Pierre was in ecstasies with Veronica's singing. When they bade her good night she came out to the door and held out her hand the second time to Duke in a excess of child-like pleasure. It had been a very happy night to her, they had been her audience and she had sung only to *them*, and had forgotten the rest of the people.

Whether it was her unconventional, trusting manner, or the extremely youthful form, he could not tell, but Duke could only look upon her as a child—still like the little singer in the streets of Florence—and he stooped and kissed the beautiful lips.

Two days later Pierre Lecroix joined the ranks of a volunteer regiment to assist in the war against Germany, and Duke flung himself into it with as much enthusiasm as a desperate man could command.

CHAPTER VI

Florence Denver was puzzled. Duke had gone away so suddenly and had scarcely given any explanation; she knew that someone was very ill and that was all. Duke had told her so with poorly feigned unconcern, but his face had contradicted it, and she knew that it was a deeper grief to him than he would admit.

William Denver was pained to see him go away again and felt that he was going to lose him just as he had flattered himself that the boy had had enough of "that confounded Paris with all its works and pomps."

Florence had loved to hold counsel with Duke about her little fears and troubles, Milton was so very reticent and Mrs. Grey was like a beautiful but sealed book to her, and she was terribly afraid that Milton was falling in love. The time for his return to college had come and gone and he did not seem to notice it.

Mrs. Grey was, if possible, sweeter and kinder than ever, but she very plainly avoided Milton. Florence would fain have asked her about the matter, but there was always a something in her manner that forbade any approach to it, and she knew that the strangely silent woman could never be questioned on any subject relating to herself.

Mrs. Grey had spoken lately about going away. Kataline could be sent to school now, and she gently intimated that her presence would be no longer necessary. After that Milton seemed to watch her movements more closely, and availed himself of the smallest excuse to see and speak to her, but she gave him little opportunity to do so, until one day when Florence had driven to the depot in the next town to meet Harold Hereford, who was coming to spend a week at the farm.

Milton had seen Mrs. Grey walking in the garden alone. She had done so since the spring days had come; she loved to watch the tender green grass, that commenced to peep above the ground, and the budding trees that already showed a dim coloring of green.

She was standing at the farthest end of the garden, gazing out upon the bleak expanse of country that had not yet commenced to don its spring garb. She seemed to be taking a long, last look at everything, and when she turned to retrace her steps, there were tears in her eyes. Milton was walking straight towards her; he was sorry to hear her speak of going away, and at once attributed her tears to that cause. With this thought in his mind, he said "I hope you are not going to leave us, Mrs. Grey, we would all miss you very much."

She looked at him through the mist in her eyes, and said quietly, "I shall be sorry to go. I have been very happy here, but the time has come when I must return to my home." They were walking towards the house now, and he stopped and said, "Will you walk with me a little more? I am also going away very soon."

"You are going back to college?" she said.

"No," he replied, "I am not going back."

"Not going back," she answered with a good deal of surprise in her face, "not going to finish your studies?"

"No, Mrs. Grey," he replied, smiling. "I have lost my vocation. I would make but a sorry churchman, at best, and I have given up the notion entirely."

Mrs. Grey was not a Catholic, but she had a deep reverence for churchmen of any denomination, and regarded any defection of this kind as little short of sacrilege.

5

"Oh, no;" she said in a protesting way, "you must not give up so easily." She was looking at him with beseeching eyes, and there was a weak quavering note in her voice. "It was your own choice," she continued, "and you will never be happy in any other path of life, and I think you will return to it after—after—awhile." She seemed to substitute the *while* for something else that was in her thoughts just then.

"I don't think so," he replied. "I was never an enthusiast about the matter. I shall never be a priest," he said, turning and standing directly in front of her, "because I *love you*, Mrs. Grey."

She must have known what was coming, and had been prepared for it, because her answer was too methodical, and came readily and coldly:

"I am very sorry for this, Mr. Denver, because I do not love you."

Her answer did not seem to surprise him, and there was a cool determination in his manner as his hand closed with a tighter pressure upon hers. He did not seem disposed to take this for an answer, because he did not believe her.

She was a strange woman in all her ways, and he had half expected that she would also be different from other women in her love affairs. He understood her enough to know that begging or pleading with her would be utterly useless; that a stronger will than her own would be the only power that she would submit to.

To anyone else her answer would have seemed an unnecessarily heartless one, but he did not think of it in that way, because he did not believe it, and he was certain that she was holding a powerful rein upon her feelings.

"I must go into the house," she said, "Kataline is alone;" and she tried to release her hand, which he still held, but he raised it and held it now closely against his bosom.

"Kataline is all right," he said, very coolly, "I hear her at the piano. *You shall not go until you tell me the truth.*"

There was a quiet, but powerful mastery in his voice, which she seemed to feel, and when he said, "We will walk a little longer," she turned, without a word, and walked very submissively beside him. When they had reached the end of the walk, he turned and faced her again, looking steadily into the eyes which she tried in vain to avert from him.

"Madeline, I will not take that answer. You are a truthful woman, and *that* was not the truth." There was not an atom of entreaty in his tone. It was more like a command.

"What is not true?" she answered weakly. "I have told you nothing but the truth."

He could see that she was only trying to gain time to parry; that she knew very well what he meant, but he gave her no time.

"You said a moment ago that you did not love me; *that* was not true. I know that you love me, and I want you to say so." He was holding both her hands so tightly that they must have hurt her, and kept his eyes upon her almost sternly.

"I dare not. It would do no good," she almost wailed, letting her head fall upon her bosom.

"But you *do* love me," he persisted, in the same unchanged voice, "and you will tell me so now."

Her answer, which came slowly, was like an effort born of infinite pain, and he had to bend low to catch it.

"Yes; but——"

His cruel grasp upon her hands relaxed in an instant,
and his arms were around her, drawing her closely to him.

"But it is useless," she began again; "I cannot—there
is——" but his lips prevented her from saying more.

"I don't care what you say, my love; I don't care what
the trouble is; I don't want to hear it.   You love me, and
that will make everything right."

He little knew that because she loved him it would make
everything wrong and wretched, that it was what she had
most dreaded, and had sought to avoid; that because of
it her life would henceforth be, not one of happiness, but
of incurable pain.

They had entered the house now, and he led her to
a chair in the parlor; she could not have stood a moment
longer, and she sank into it in sheer exhaustion.   He
brought a chair and sat near her, holding one of her hands
fondly in his.

"You are not sorry for telling me the truth, my darling,"
he said, raising her hand to his lips.

"But you are to enter the church," she said, after a
little silence.   "What would the world say of you and of
me?   Is it not considered, in your community, a sort of
disgrace to combat or renounce your vocation?"

"I believe so," he said, a little impatiently, "but *that*
comes of our being so much a community of one idea.
If we were less so, we would be much happier.   What is
the world to you and me, Madeline?" he continued
warmly.   "Why should its opinions hinder our happiness,
or hem us in?   If you were my wife, I could laugh at the
worst verdict the world could give.   We would be happy
enough to defy ten worlds."

"But we cannot," she replied sadly; "we cannot
always do what our hearts dictate."

"We *have* a right to do what our hearts dictate. We should make our own world, and if we did, the other one would soon forget us."

Mrs. Grey was standing now, and was nervously folding and unfolding a scrap of paper, which she had taken from the table.

"Your family, your father would never forgive me," she said slowly. "They want you to be a priest; I can never marry you, Milton." She had moved away from him, as if to gather strength to say this. Whatever were her reasons for refusing him, this was plainly but an excuse with which she tried to conceal the real cause.

An impatient answer rose to his lips, but he repressed it, as he saw the terrible depth of pain in her eyes. He followed her, and took her hands again. "That is all nonsense, Madeline," he said; "thousands of men have done the same. The Catholic Church does not want luke-warm apostles, neither is it a tyrant that compels unwilling votaries. I am my own master, and shall choose for myself. You shall be my wife, Madeline, and I will take no refusal."

The noise of wheels warned them that Florence and Harold Hereford had returned. Mrs. Grey made a movement to leave the room, and he released her hand suddenly, only to put both arms around her for a moment, holding her close to him, and then let her go.

When she was gone, he stooped and picked up the scrap of crumpled paper which she had dropped. It was a twisted unsightly thing, but every fold and crease could tell more of mental misery, more of despair, than words could ever have told.

Mrs. Grey went quickly to her room; she was glad to get away. Her heart had been forming answers to his arguments, but she could not utter them while he was there looking at her. It was only of *his* happiness that she thought now—there could be none for *her*. She should let her hidden love burn itself out, even though it consumed her life. To keep suffering away from him, to convince him by some clever argument that they would be better apart, were the things paramount in her thoughts.

Whatever her miserable secret was, it confronted her now like a hideous spectre, and stood grimly between her and her happiness—pointing with a warning finger to the danger lying in her path. She sat in the window, staring with wide, dry eyes into the night, fighting the miserable battle that had *self* for an opponent—and self was triumphant, and a heart-beaten woman left the window only when the first faint streaks in the east warned her that it was morning.

There was wonderful sunshine in Florence's face next morning, when she came into Mrs. Grey's room and kissed her in bed.

"Do you know that *someone* came last night?" she said. "Try and guess who."

"Oh, easy enough to guess, my dear," said Mrs. Grey. "How long is 'somebody' going to stay?"

"Oh, maybe a week—perhaps a *whole* day—one can never tell anything about *his* movements."

"Florence," said Mrs. Grey, after a pause, and she made an effort to look cheerful, "I must begin to think about going away very soon. Now don't say anything against it, dear," she added, smiling, and putting her hand over Florence's mouth; "mamma is getting quite anxious for my return."

Florence's face fell upon hearing this. They had come to look upon Mrs. Grey as a member of the family, and they were anxious that she should remain with them. Florence was thoughtful for awhile, and when she spoke there was an unusual note of quiet resolution in her voice.

"Mrs. Grey, has—will you tell me has Milton ——" She had struck the right key, and before she could finish, Mrs. Grey answered quickly, "Yes, Florence, he has—and now you know, dear," she added faintly, "that it is time to go."

Florence arose silently, but stooped again and kissed the pale face, without a word, and left the room.

Mrs. Grey complained of a headache, and did not leave her room that day. Next morning, when Milton and Harold had gone to the next town, she arose and walked with Florence in the garden. They were both very silent as people usually are who have much to say upon a subject that both are loth to mention. It was a splendid spring morning, and one could almost see the soft green buds unfolding, and the tender grass springing beneath their feet.

Mrs. Grey's eyes were humid, and she seemed to look at things as if she was never to see them again—the trees and plants and promised flowers that she was never to see in bloom. They were about to return to the house—neither of them having the courage to speak of the matter which was uppermost in their thoughts. The noise of wheels announced that Milton and Harold had returned, and they had not reached the house before the young men had seen them. Another moment and Milton was saying: "Mrs. Grey, I believe you have not met Dr. Hereford."

It was well for Mrs. Grey that neither Milton nor Florence could see her face just then, and Harold looked for a moment as if he had seen a ghost. Mrs. Grey looked at him with tightly-closed lips, and he seemed to understand that she was imploring silence. Then Harold tried to say

something pleasant, and they both regained composure
without being noticed.   In a little while they all returned
to the house.   They made a pretense of playing and singing a little, but there seemed to be a weight upon everyone's
spirits, and they soon gave it up.

Mrs. Grey escaped to her room before the lights were
brought, and did not join them at supper.   This woman's
misery had now reached its zenith.   An hour later she lay
prone upon the floor of her room, despairing and defeated.

From her window she saw Dr. Hereford in the garden,
next morning, and went quietly out there and joined him.

He came quickly towards her, noting the terrible change
in her face since yesterday.   When they had walked far
enough from the house, she turned a beseeching face to
him, and said hurriedly, " You will not tell them?   You
will have pity on me, will you not?   I am going away, and
they will never see me again.   I should have gone long
before now, but it is so hard.   I have been almost happy
here. But I am going now, only spare me," she continued
piteously, "and they shall never hear of me again."

"Yes, Miriam Walton," he said gently, " you will have
to go away, and at once. If Milton had not——" Here she
laid a hand upon his arm, saying, " Florence has told you
that ?

" Yes," he answered, "she has told me.   Only for
that——"

" Yes," she interrupted, "only for *that.*"

" I have tried to find you," he resumed, after a painful
pause, "but never thought of finding you here.   That
name," he added, hesitatingly—"Yes," she replied, "my
mother's.   I thought it best."

" I am very sorry for you," he said, " but you know there
no alternative. You must go at once, and never let them
know where you are."

"Yes," she said, more as if following out a train of thought, than in reply to him, "I must go away, and never let them know where I am. Is—is there no hope for me?" she asked, weakly.

"Oh, yes—certainly," he replied, hastily, "but it will take time—perhaps years. I will do all that I can for you, if you will let me know where to find you."

"You are very good, Dr. Hereford," she replied; "and you promise not to tell them? Oh, it would be dreadful," she continued, clasping her hands together, "to let them know that all this time they have had such a thing as I am amongst them."

"They shall never know, Mrs. Walton," he said kindly, "and if you wish to go to-morrow, I will take Milton away for the day. Don't you think it would be better so?"

She answered mechanically, "Yes, it would be better so; take him away."

At this moment they saw Milton coming towards them, laughing and saying, "that he was getting abominably jealous; another instance of the 'early bird,'" he added; but his face fell when he saw the misery in Mrs. Grey's, and the grave expression upon Harold's.

"Hereford," he said, trying to look cheerful, "Florence wants the assistance you promised her last night, in the new-fangled creation of coffee—she awaits your highness in the kitchen."

"All right," Harold replied, "make Mrs. Grey continue her walk, she has her headache still," and he left them.

When he had gone, Milton looked at her long and searchingly. "You are ill, my darling," he said.

"Only a headache," she answered; "it is getting better."

"What has Dr. Hereford been saying to you, and why

did you both look so grave this morning? You seem like old friends, too," he added, with a little touch of resentment in his voice.

"Yes," she answered evasively, "I knew him many years ago; but you have no right to be jealous," she added, trying to turn the conversation into a cheerful channel, "as long as Florence is not."

"Oh, that shows that Florence is not as much in love as I am," he said; "if she *were*, she would not have been so magnanimous about lending her lover to *you* this morning."

"It shows that she has good sense, not to be jealous of an old woman like me," she answered with a faint smile.

She was making a supreme effort to appear cheerful. It was an Herculean task, when she felt like one who was standing upon the verge of her grave, looking death in the face, and actually feeling its cold current in her veins; even with all her youth and beauty, with a man close to her for whom her heart was full of love, who might bring sunshine and happiness into her darkened life, could she but *dare*—but the hideous spectre that followed her had said *no*, and she must per force obey it.

Kataline came to announce breakfast, and they returned to the house with her.

Harold took Milton away to a distant farm next day, to visit some old friends of his, and Mrs. Grey was thus given the opportunity which she desired. Florence and she had agreed that it was better not to let Milton know of her departure. Florence could tell him that she had been sent for hurriedly, and that she had promised to write to him.

Florence was grieved, and her father, who little suspected the under-current of things, was satisfied only when she had promised to come back again. She had become closely interwoven in their affections and they found it difficult to part. The two women had agreed that it was better, and Florence had a secret hope that Milton would return to college when she was gone.

Milton was terribly disappointed when he came home in the evening and found that Mrs. Grey had gone. He waited anxiously for the promised letter but it did not come, and then, in spite of all remonstrances, he started in search of her, and they saw nothing of him for a week. At the end of that time he came back, appearing like a ghost at Harold's door one night, as he was about to retire to bed.

Harold asked him kindly if he had seen Mrs. Grey. He had flung himself into a chair and answered with a sullen "*No!*" After that he remained silent for a long time with his head bowed upon his hands—a thousand improbable fancies were rushing through his brain. What was the matter?—had she hidden from him that one short week had seemed to him like an eternity? She might be sick, perhaps dying; and now, also, the memory came back to him of the trouble he had seen in her face the morning he had found her walking with Harold in the garden, and out of this grew a suspicion that Harold had something to do with her going away, and now he flamed up angrily and said: "I think you know something about her, Hereford; tell me what you know."

Harold was very sorry for his friend, but hardly knew what to say; in fact there was but very little that *he could* say under the circumstances. He did not expect this question and he hesitated before answering it, which made the other still more suspicious.

"Yes, you know where she is," he added, "and you are hiding it from me."

Harold had no idea that Milton's feeling for Mrs. Grey had been anything more than a mere fancy that would die out when she had gone away. He would rather not have told him what he knew of her, and besides he felt bound to keep, in a measure, his promise to her. To guard against the possibility of her return to the farm he had been obliged to give Florence some reason, and he had told her simply that Mrs. Grey was not a fit person to live among them, and she did not question him further. But here was something that he had not calculated upon—the young man before him was in a desperate mood and must be answered. He saw also now that any attempt at concealment would only make matters worse; it must be told to him, he thought, and he will then become disenchanted with his unhappy idol.

"Milton," he said, in a very gentle voice, "Mrs. Grey was not a fit person to live in this house."

This was like putting a match to a smouldering fire. Milton was aflame instantly and before Harold knew what he was about he had struck at him with his clenched hand.

"It is a lie," he shouted, "an infamous lie, and you have a purpose in telling it; you drove her away and you will find her by ——"

"Come out of here, Milton," begged Harold. "Come out where Florence will not hear us, and I will tell you all I know of this." He put on his slippers, and Milton went out before him without a word.

"Now, sir," queried Milton, when they had reached the garden, "tell me quick, and no more of your confounded lies—tell me where she is."

Harold kept his temper, and still spoke in the same even tone: "*Mrs. Grey is a dangerous lunatic, and has been under my care for a year.*"

But he found that he was talking to a man who was determined not to believe him; his great love for this woman had blinded him to all reason.

"You are a liar and a coward, Harold Hereford, and *you are in love with her yourself.* You know where she is, and if you do not tell me, I will kill you."

It made no matter now that those two had been children together, had been companions at school, and as men, had been the warmest friends. Love and friendship were swept entirely away by the demons of anger and jealousy.

Harold, who was the coolest and most forbearing, saw now that there was little use in arguing the matter any further, anything more that he could say—and there was worse still to be told—would not help matters any, so he said as quietly as he could, "I have nothing more to say, Milton; I have told you the truth, and you are determined not to believe me."

He did not want to quarrel with his old friend and schoolfellow, he had taken no notice of the unjust names that he had applied to him, his better judgment telling him that it would be best to seemingly submit to anything that Milton, in his present mood, would say. "You have wronged me," he continued, "but you will find out that I am not deceiving you."

But the other was getting more exasperated by the coolness which Harold showed, and burst in with, "I don't believe a word you say, and if you are not a worse coward than I take you for you will *meet me in the morning.*"

"Very well," Harold replied in the same even voice, "any place you wish."

"The Hill field will do," answered Milton sullenly, "what have you?"

"Colt's."

"All right," answered Milton, "I'll find one. Five
o'clock," he called back, as he turned on his heel and disap-
peared in the darkness.

Harold bitterly regretted the turn that affairs had taken,
and was sorry that he had not taken Florence into
his confidence, and told her the truth concerning
Mrs. Grey.   Milton might have believed *her*, but
he certainly would believe neither of them *now*.   He
went to his room and arranged his affairs as one might
who was certain of death in the morning.   He cared little
for his own life, and the greatest regret he would have in
dying was for the gentle girl, who was to have been his
wife in a few months.   It was hard to die because of this,
and he knew that in his present temper, Milton would try
to kill him, and he had resolved that he would not touch a
hair of Milton's head.

He was a brave man and was capable of making a generous sacrifice, and he weakened only when he remembered
that he could not even say farewell to the girl whom he had
loved all his life; to hold her in his arms and kiss her for
the last time would make death less bitter.   He even
thought of calling her and making some excuse for having to
leave unexpectedly, but he dared not trust himself,
there would surely be something in his last despairing embrace that might arouse her suspicions.   No, he must deny
himself even this.

He would be obliged to go to a distant farm to procure
a young friend to act as second, and before he started he went
softly around to Florence's window and stood before it for a
minute.   During that space of time he was an abject coward.
It was the most supreme moment in his life, and the weak-
est.   He felt, while standing there, that nothing on earth
could make him go, but he recalled himself by a

desperate effort and turned sharply away, hurrying from the place; had he stayed there a moment longer his heart would have broken, and Milton would have had a bloodless satisfaction.

He arrived with his friend at the " Hill field " while it was yet almost dark, and found Milton and his friend waiting for them. The seconds, who were old friends, shook hands sadly enough. Milton handed a case containing a pair of bright, new revolvers to Harold, one of which he took and silently returned the other.

The " Hill field " was about four miles from the house and was quite secluded, bordered almost entirely around with tall trees. The shadows in the early morning were gigantic and reached far into the middle of the field—this morning they looked ominous and ghostly. There was promise of a beautiful day for the rest of the living world. The delicate streaks of crimson and cream had begun to appear in the east, and there was just light enough to show the faint fairy-like glimmering of hoar frost upon the tender young grass. The widening, glowing streaks of light shooting upwards from their gorgeous dawn-bed in the east, promised a gracious and peaceful spring day.

The few stars that still shone palely in the east seemed to twinkle a farewell and a welcome, at the same time, to the coming god of day, but these harbingers of beauty, and peace, and harmony formed a strange and incongruous frame to the ghastly picture beneath.

"Suit yourself about the distance, as near as you please," Milton had said. Before Harold allowed himself to be placed he walked up to Milton and said, "Take my hand for Florence's sake, it is the last time, and then you may kill me as soon as you please."

" No," replied Milton, savagely, " I would not touch

you; don't mention *her* name." That was all, and in
half a minute more they had faced each other, and
Milton's pistol rang out upon the air first.

Harold felt that he had been hit in the shoulder but he
did not fire. He could easily have killed his man now, but
instead, he flung his pistol away as far as he could, and kept
advancing towards Milton.

"Why don't you fire?" cried the other, angrily. "I
want no favors from you," and he backed away from him
doggedly.

"I did not come here to kill you, Milton. You can
fire again and finish your work; then, perhaps, you will
believe that I have told you the truth."

The blood was now running in a thick stream down his
arm, and his shirt-sleeve, soaked with it, was clinging to
his wrist.

Milton had not been aware that he was wounded until
now, and the sight of the blood seemed to recall him to a
more rational state of mind. A dawning sense of his blind
injustice and brutality towards his old friend, brought a
flush of remorse and shame to his face.

"Hereford, —" he began, but by this time Harold had
become so weak that he was about to fall forward had not
the young men grasped him, each by the arm, and laid
him gently on the ground.

Milton's anger-wrought feelings had now changed to
remorseful horror, as the conviction that he had killed his
old friend and school-fellow came fully upon him, and he
felt that he was a murderer.

They stanched the bleeding as well as they could, and
lifted him into the carriage, which Milton had ordered,
and which had been waiting for the grim possibility of con-
veying one or the other of them from the field.

They drove quickly to the Columbia Hotel in R——n, and the doctors pronounced the wound "not dangerous."

When Harold recovered consciousness, his first words to Milton were, " Go home quickly, and tell Florence that I had been summoned late last night to see a patient who was in danger. Lose no time, Milton," he said anxiously, "I am all right, old fellow; there, take my hand."

Milton wrung it in shame and silence, and then left him to the care of the doctors. When he arrived at the farm, he found Florence and his father in a state of painful anxiety concerning their absence. He had accompanied Harold, he said, and they had thought it best not to awaken any one, hoping to be back before morning. "Harold," he said, "might be delayed there a few days, the case being more serious than they had expected."

A letter had come for Harold that morning marked, "in haste," and Milton found it an excellent excuse for returning to R——n at once. He found Harold very much improved and in great spirits. He tried to make light of the whole thing, and persisted in laughing at Milton's very lugubrious countenance, and asserting that he was furiously hungry.

Milton was thereupon dispatched in search of some provender, and while he was gone Harold took up the letter, saying, as he looked at the envelope, " I wonder what this is!" It was a woman's hand, and strange to him. He tore it open. It ran: '

" Come, all of you. Milton and Florence come quickly in pity, I am dying. The stage will bring you in an hour to ' Harshaw's ranch.'

MADELINE GREY."

" Doctor," he said, turning to Dr. Hale, " can you fix me up for an hour's journey?"

6

"It would not be safe," he replied, "there is every danger of inflammation. I don't like——"

"But I must go," he persisted—"there is no alternative—and at once."

When Milton returned he was astonished to find Harold out of bed trying to dress himself, and arguing crossly with the doctors.

"Milton," he said, "get a mouthful of something as quickly as you can. I want you to do me another favor—I won't tell you until you have eaten something."

Milton, to please him, turned to the table which a waiter had by this time fixed in the middle of the room, and emptied a glass of sherry. "Now," he said, "your commands, my lord."

"Get a carriage, quick, Milton, and go back for Florence; we have found Mrs. Grey. Take that with you," he added, putting the letter into his hand. "Don't lose a moment."

Milton glanced at the note and saw all as if it had been but one word, and rushed from the room.

Dr. Hale, to whom Harold had confided the matter, agreed to accompany them, and Milton having arrived in a very short space of time they were all soon upon the journey to "Harshaw ranch."

They found Madeline Grey in the secluded farm-house, where she had hidden herself from the world for the last time. The stricken mother, a veritable ghost herself, was hovering around the death-bed of her only child, and came out to the door to meet them.

"Could they see her now?"

"Oh, yes, they could come in at once; she had been waiting and could not die until she had seen them."

Florence was the first to enter the sick-room and the

pitiable, wan face brightened wonderfully when she saw her. Then Harold came, but her eyes did not rest upon him, but looked past him into the hallway. She could see Milton away out there, and could read the agony upon his face. He was coming in, and she held her arms out to him, her eyes full of love and pity.

"There is nothing to come between us now, my darling," she murmured, as he bent over her. "Oh, why did you go away from me!" was all that he could say. "You shall *not* die; you shall come home with us now."

The dying woman smiled sadly into his eyes. "No," she said, "but you will stay with me to the last. My life will be short now, but it will be very happy, because you are here with me." He had raised her up and was holding her in his arms. The end was, indeed, very near, but he would not believe it, she looked so radiantly happy.

"I have had such a troubled life," she said, "but it is gone now forever, and I am oh, so happy, and you will be glad," she said softly, stroking his hair, "because I died so happily—but tell me," she added, imploringly, "that you have not been angry with Dr. Hereford. I dreamed last night that there was some—some trouble—" Here she glanced from one to the other with the keen perception of the dying, and guessed what they would have given worlds to hide.

"Come here, Florence," she said, in a voice that was now wonderfully strong and clear, "and you, Dr. Hereford—I have not strength to tell them. I want you to explain—to—to—tell them *what I* have been—what I *am*. You will not?" she said, seeing his head droop, "then I will have to do it, but, oh," she added shuddering, "it is hard to tell. Wait until I am dead, Dr. Hereford, and then it will be—but no," she resumed in a calmer voice, "it is better that *I* should tell it. Florence, Milton, *I have been an unhappy lunatic for more than five years.* It was inherited from my poor father, and I was not aware that *I* had the terrible malady, until after my marriage, when my first child was born. When it was a year old," here a terrible spasm of pain crossed her face, " I *destroyed* it, and —and a few months afterwards," here she looked appealingly at Dr. Hereford, but he only said, " There is nothing more to tell, Mrs. Grey, nothing more." "Oh, yes," she answered, "this—*this*, that I destroyed *my husband also.*"

" My poor darling," said Milton, " why speak of these things? Your cure is almost complete now. Dr. Hereford," he added, looking appealingly to him, " says, that it has nearly died out—and——"

" Yes, my poor love," she interrupted, " I am all right until I *love—that is my madness. I want to kill the beings that I love most.* Had I never met you—" here her arms closed around Milton's neck. The poor, over-strained heart drank in one last, long draught of happiness, and then—must have broken. When Milton raised his head again, there was a sweet smile upon her dead lips.

CHAPTER VII.

A year had passed away. Milton had gone back to college, and was about to fulfill the dearest wish of Florence's heart by preparing for his ordination.

It was within three months of Florence's wedding, and the old farm-house was gaily alive with preparations. Kataline was masquerading in Florence's bridal dress and sailed demurely up to her father, who had grown very gray of late, and his eyes filled with tears as he kissed the mock bride, and then she was captured by Florence just in time to save the magnificent train from being tampered with by an irrepressible cat.

There was only one shadow upon Florence's happiness lately—it was that there was no letter from Duke. They had heard of his career from the papers—a brilliant one—and of the honors which would have been heaped upon him, had he cared for them.

They were proud of his deeds, and did not know of the despairing recklessness which had given birth to them.

The war of 1870–71 was over, and the sun shone as brightly on the blood-stained fields of France, as if it had never happened.

Duke and his friend were back again in Paris, beaten, tear-stained, but still living—Paris, in which the conquerors were still revelling over their victory.

The excitement of war had been a sort of buoy that held Duke from sinking in the ocean of his sorrow, but now that it was over the old vacuum in his heart made itself felt again, and he could almost have wished that it had lasted longer, for even that which had brought sorrow and

death to many, had brought at least oblivion, to him.
Paris now indeed was like a huge sepulchre, it was the
grave of his happiness.

In his grief for his country's defeat, Pierre Lacroix had
ignored an ugly sword cut upon his arm, and his great,
loving heart and brain were already planning a new ruse
whereby he would courageously "take the bull by the
horns," and strangle this beast of melancholy, which had
so fatal a hold upon his blithe young friend, and when
things looked the most hopeless to the vivacious young
Frenchman, he was wont to infuse a dash of desperation
into his plans, and could thereby actually accomplish
seemingly impossible things.

"What are you going to do, Pierre?" said Duke, a few
days after they had arrived in Paris. "What are your
plans *de campagne* now?"

This was exactly the opening Pierre had wished for, and
he replied briskly, " You mean, what are *we* going to do,
mon comrade. Remember that *we* are artist brothers, soldier brothers, brothers in misfortune, brothers in *everything*.
I refuse to be separated from you. I cannot work without
you. You have become, in fact, my necessary sail—devil,
if you like. I cannot *live* without you, and shall not leave
you unless you kick me out; and you will *have* to kick me
before I go."

Duke could not help laughing. It was all said in the
Frenchman's own serio-comic style, but there was an un-
mistakable chord of seriousness ringing in every word.

" Very well, Pierre," said Duke, " but I shall be sorry
to burden your life with such gruesome companionship as
mine is sure to be, but you won't be able to endure it very
long, and then you are at liberty to kick *me* out."

" *Laboremus*," said Pierre, meditatively, as if he had not

noticed Duke's reply, " *that* is the watchword *now*. *Mon Dieu!*" he murmured still to himself. " We *must* work. We are homeless beggars, beaten soldiers. We are nothing. Let us be something. We are nobodies, and have no right even to growl. Let us be something, first, and then growl because we are not greater."

Duke laughed until his heart really felt lighter, and they did not go to bed that night until he had succeeded in making Duke take an interest in the earnest work which they were about to commence at once.

" *Work* is the thing for him—the very best medicine," thought Pierre, " and I will keep him hard at it; and my name is not Lacroix if I give him time to think."

Pierre had also cautiously and cunningly instituted a short disquisition now and then upon the subject of melancholy, adroitly substituting Veronica Venella as an example. Only a loving heart could conceive the ruse.

Duke had not yet visited Pere-la-Chaise. In fact, he could not escape long enough from Pierre to go there alone, Pierre having magnanimously promised to accompany him "when he could spare time," and resolutely ignored the fact that Duke would have preferred to go alone. In his inmost heart Duke had felt obliged to accuse him of a slight want of delicacy in this matter, but he said nothing. War makes men regardless of the finer feelings, and Pierre, he thought, must certainly have lost much of the consideration which he had had for his— Duke's—feelings.

And strangely, too, it was not of Duke's grief that he talked now, it was of Veronica's. He never seemed to think of Duke's loss any more, it was always of Veronica's; he talked about it night after night, depicting in sorrowful colors the loss of the poor girl's only friend in the death of the princess. Now, indeed, he spoke of the princess only in relation to her lovely *protege*. It was no longer the woman who had died for love of Duke Denver, and there was nothing to be regretted *now* but the heart-breaking of the tender girl who had been loved and cared for by her.

Pierre could draw the most pathetic pictures of the sorrows of the girl thus rudely severed from her bene-factress and thrown now, no doubt, among an element which must surely be repugnant to her exquisite feel-ings. He (Pierre) could not bear to go to Pere-la-Chaise and find her; they would be sure to find her there weeping the life out of her young heart, and why should they, strong fellows, yet with plenty of work in them, worry about anything. Should they not rather do something to save this gentle child from the grave which her grief was surely digging for her? They should at least try. Poor Veronica!

His plans were succeeding admirably. By continually striking upon the sad chord in Duke's heart he had almost deadened it, and had fully awakened his sympathies for Veronica.

Duke was forgetting his own sorrow; he would now, indeed, be ashamed to have pitted it against that of the girl whose life must have been a very sad one since.

" It seems strange," said Duke, one day, "how we had almost forgotten her."

" *I* never forgot her," answered Pierre, loftily. " I thought of her very often, indeed, and I am anxious to see her again, *very* anxious," he continued, with a furtive glance at Duke.

The other looked at him, wonderingly, but said nothing. One day, when he thought he had escaped the lynx eye of Pierre, he went to the cemetery with more of the lonely

Veronica in his thoughts than had ever been there before. He might have gone to her house, but a feeling that he should like to meet her again at the grave seemed to influence him. He had been thinking about her a good deal lately, and Pierre's eloquent portrayal of her sorrow had wrought powerfully upon his kindly heart, and he felt, indeed, that he would have been very much disappointed if he did not find her in Pere-la-Chaise that day, and the hope grew stronger until it outweighed the motives that had hitherto drawn him there.

The evening shadows were dimming the dazzling whiteness of the marble in Pere-la-Chaise. When he found himself again at the cherished grave a great wave of grief swept over him, opening afresh the miserable wound in his heart. A feeling that Veronica was near, that she would surely come to share his grief, had in it a sort of balm. When he had breathed a reverent prayer for the beloved dead he thought again of the young face which he had kissed here over the grave, and he was glad that he had kissed her, although it had been a somewhat selfish act on his part *then*—it was as if he would rob her of the last kiss which the dear dead lips had left there, but he was glad *now* that he had done it and thought, too, that if he should ever kiss her again it would be more for Veronica's sake than that of the loved one gone.

It had grown dark, and he had not noticed it. He was still standing there in deep thought, when two women approached the grave. He felt sure that one of them must be Veronica. Would she recognize him was his first thought. He knew that he was very much changed. He was standing in the deepest shadow, so that they could scarcely see him until they had come very close. Veronica, for it was she, was talking to the older woman, who was evidently her mother, and her voice, he thought, had sad notes in it like the music of an Æolian harp, and it thrilled him as he listened.

Veronica laid some flowers upon the tomb, and in doing so, saw him, and started back in affright, but it was only for a second, and then she went quickly around to where he stood—even in the dim light she had recognized him—then she stopped, as if ashamed of her boldness, and murmured falteringly:

"Monsieur Denver?"

They were only a few feet apart now, and he opened his arms without a word, but there was a world of love and joy in his eyes, and a prayer of deep thankfulness in his heart, as she went straight into his arms, and laid her face against his bosom.

Truly, across that holy grave the unseen chain of love had at last linked those two young hearts together.

When he had, as he thought, outwitted Pierre that day, and had succeeded on reaching the cemetery alone, that individual had been perfectly cognizant of his doings, and when Duke was clearly out of sight, he proceeded to indulge in a grin of such diabolical nature and dimensions as would have astonished anyone who had the luck to witness it. His "prophetic powers," which were coming into play again, told him that Veronica would be in the cemetery, and that Duke would be sure to meet her there. Had Duke gone any place else *but there* he would have been anxious and impatient for his return, but he sat now smoking contentedly, seeing wonderful pictures in the smoke-wreaths in which Duke and Veronica were the happy figures.

Duke came home late that night, with a rather bashful air, and a very happy light in his eyes, upon seeing which

Pierre proceeded to behave himself in an atrocious and unaccountable manner. First, he sent his shoe through the canvas, upon which he had worked industriously the day before, upon a head of Petrarch.

He then put on his boxing gloves and sparred furiously at Duke, who knew nothing of the noble art, until he, Duke, was sore all over. When he had tired of that, he practiced the "William Tell trick" upon a valued bust of Chaucer, and was seemingly overjoyed when he succeeded in knocking the nose off. If it was exuberance of spirits— Duke thought it was brandy—he ought to have been satisfied by this time, but to Duke's alarm, when the landlord came up to enquire what all the noise was about, Pierre ordered a supper which would have appalled a millionaire— ordered it with the air of a prince—and concluded by making the landlord, a venerable old man of sixty years, stoop, while he performed a complicated feat of leap-frog over him. After that, he sat down, from sheer exhaustion, and dropped into a meditative mood, which lasted until the supper was announced, and which he ate with as much gusto as if he knew how it was going to be paid for.

"Eat, my friend," he said, waving his hand towards Duke. "We are but creatures of the moment; let us enjoy each one as if it were to be the last. What do we know about a future? Why worry about it? Who can assure us of an hour's existence? Then let us get all we can out of the present one. Fall to, man," seeing that Duke was regarding "the lay-out" with a stare of dismay. "It is the rich," he continued, "who should fast, the gourmand, the glutton, the gorged. Why should we not feast? What is left to us when luck fails us? An appetite! When the fortunes of war go against us, when love is denied us, when friends desert us, what stays with us? Oh, what indeed, but our faithful appetites? They cheer and console us, and lift us out of the mire of melancholy. Here's to the appetite, Duke, let us respect it. Fill your glass, old man—more—more—fill it to the brim. Now, then, if we die to-morrow," he continued, laying down his empty glass, "we shall die like gentlemen, and let the devil pay the piper."

When the table had been cleared away, and they had settled down for a comfortable smoke, the little Frenchman grew very serious, and again relapsed into deep thought.

"What are you thinking about now, Pierre?" said Duke, "trying to sift some sense out of all that nonsense?"

"Yes, and no," replied Pierre. "I was just wondering if I could persuade some woman to marry me. I'm getting old and lonely, *mon comrade,*" he added, with a sigh, "and am, in fact, tired of myself. Now, if I belonged to somebody else—to some nice woman, for instance, I would begin to set some value upon myself again; in fact, I would take a little more interest in the respectable married Monsieur Lacroix."

"What are you going to do with me?" Duke asked, laughing. "If you cast me out what will become of me?"

"Go and do likewise," Pierre replied, with a grin. "If you don't, you are no longer respectable in *my* eyes. A man without a wife is an incomplete animal at best—an incomplete animal, and should have no consideration. He is a useless spoke in the world's wheel, a soulless, selfish, loveless weight. Duke," he said, changing his tone suddenly, "whom did you see to-day?"

Duke blushed to the roots of his hair, but he answered simply, "Veronica."

"Veronica," echoed Pierre, "alive and well. I was

afraid something might have happened to her," here two great big tears actually rolled down his face, "and we had almost forgotten her—beasts." Duke could not resist the great womanish tears and they unlocked the secret which he would have hidden a little longer. "She is alive and well, Pierre," he said, his eyes shining with a suspicious moisture, "and—and——"

"And she has consented to marry you, you dear old goose," Pierre shouted; "you beloved old sneak, and you are going to desert *me*, you unfaithful wretch, and I am the man with the 'broken heart' *now*." He was holding Duke around the neck with a grip that tightened with each word and he let go only when Duke reminded him that he did not wish to die of strangulation. Then he released him rather reluctantly and went to see if there was anything left to drink to Veronica's health and then he sat down and vowed that he was "going to be an American."

"Duke," he said, quite seriously, "don't all your great men begin by being beggars, or backwoods men, or something of that sort? I want to begin life all over again. I want to be *re-born* in America and thereby become a sort of cousin to you, *mon ami*."

"All right, old man, you *shall*," replied Duke, "you shall come over there with me, and begin your great career as soon as you please."

And it turned out that there were two weddings instead of one at the farm, and Pierre and Veronica's mother were there, and they go over regularly every year and spend three months there, and William Denver is the happiest old man in the country because his favorite boy has given up the "crazy picture business," and settled down to "decent farm life," and moreover he had the sweetest little wife in the world.

When Florence and her husband came to visit them they compared babies, which were always ridiculously alike in looks and years, and such occasions were generally like Fourth of July celebrations on a small scale.

And there is forever enshrined in the hearts of the young farmer and his wife, a saint, whose grave is in Pere-la-Chaise, and their memory of her has become a holy reverence into which grief and regret no longer enter.

The mother of Madeline Grey did not long survive the death of her unfortunate child, and William Denver provided comfortably for her remaining years.

Only a Tramp.

"Why Ella, child, what *have* you been doing?" exclaimed Mrs. Winter, raising her hands and eyebrows in mild surprise, as a beautiful girl stood before her with an armful of flowers. Great crimson roses mingled their dewy loveliness with pure white ones, and velvet pansies lay with their faces half hidden beneath a tangle of heliotrope and smilax.

"Oh, these are for Willie, mamma!" replied the fair culprit, laying her beautiful burden upon a table, and she picked out a yellow rosebud, which well deserved its name, "Gold of Ophir," and pinned it in her mother's bosom—an act which immediately disarmed the old lady of rising displeasure, Ella's depredations among her beloved flowers being of frequent occurrence.

Mrs. Winter had been a widow for many years, her husband, a California miner, having, in mining parlance, "passed in his checks," leaving her in comfortable circumstances, and she lived a secluded life, with her only child, in a pretty suburb of San Francisco.

Willie Gaynor was a distant cousin, whom Ella had never seen, but she was almost in love with a handsome boyish face, which looked at her from an old daguerreotype upon the mantelpiece, and whose somewhat saucy mouth she had often furtively kissed. His father had written that he was coming to spend a vacation with them.

"I trust, dear Margaret," ran the letter, "that he shall be the link which will unite again the chain of our long severed, but never forgotten friendship."

And now Ella was about to behold her girlish ideal, whom her imagination had so often pictured!

He lived "away up" in the mountains where they disembowelled the earth of its golden treasures, and to Ella's romantic mind must belong to the primitive heroes depicted by Joaquin Miller and Prentice Mulford.

To-day was a very happy one for Ella. The sun was certainly brighter, the flowers had a sweeter perfume, and seemed to have gained more radiant colors. They are waiting for a letter, which would tell the time of his arrival. Ella gazes expectantly towards the gate, and is at last rewarded by the appearance of the gray-coated postman, whose homely face looks positively handsome to her this morning. With a dexterous twist of finger and thumb, "the result of constant practice," he sends a letter flying up the garden path, and as Ella runs lightly towards him, it lands softly and significantly against her lips, and then drops at her feet. She picked it up with a blush, which put all the pretentious pink flowers in the garden to shame.

The letter is for *her* this time—the first she has ever received from her cousin, and her hands tremble as she tears open the envelope. She walked back through the garden slowly, and Mrs Winter coming to the window is just in time to see the joyous, expectant look die out of her face, and an expression of the deepest disappointment succeed the happy one which brightened it a moment ago.

"Oh, mamma, Willie says he cannot leave for a month. I'm so sorry." There is a sad cadence in her voice as she softly utters the word "sorry," which would have told

Mr. Gaynor a good deal could he have heard it. A great big sigh accompanied her words, as she looked regretfully at the flowers which she had gathered especially for him, and which now seemed to droop their lovely heads in unison with her sorrow, but young hearts are made of very elastic material, and blithesome Ella was soon herself again.

I hope my reader will not find fault with my heroine when I disclose the fact that she never tried to conceal a strong partiality for dogs. They were her playmates and faithful protectors in childhood and all of the dignity of young ladyhood lacked power to banish them from her side now. Great, shaggy fellows, with big, affectionate brown eyes, were her especial favorites, but every canine, from the petted pug to the slim and graceful greyhound, had a place in her affections, but in all her life she never had occasion to find fault with any of them until to-day, when her prime favorite covered her with shame and humiliation.

This is how it happened: Donning her big sunhat and calling her pet, Nigger, and a small specimen named Ruby, she sallied forth for her usual ramble, with spirits as light as if the disappointment of the morning had never occurred. All went well until Nigger encountered a casual acquaintance, in the shape of a pugilistic-looking black dog, who was evidently on the "war-path." He sniffed around Nigger for a few moments and then threw down the glove, so to speak. Nigger, to his eternal disgrace, lent an unwilling ear to the agonized entreaties of his young mistress, wavered just a moment and then "went for his opponent with a vim which promised to make 'things lively' all around." The "small specimen" made a few spasmodic dashes toward the combatants, but deeming "discretion the better part of valor" in this case, sat down at a safe distance and watched the fight uneasily.

Ella is in despair and looks vainly around for help; espying a stick she picks it up and pokes aimlessly at the dogs, in a futile effort to separate them. She has just given up all hope, when, to her great relief, a man appears upon the scene. He is grimy and ragged, but she takes no notice of it, but begs him, earnestly, to save her pet from the monster who is bent upon devouring him. An amused smile flickers around the man's mouth for an instant as he looks at her, then grasping a dog with each hand, he flings one clear over the fence and is about to fling the other in an opposite direction, but Ella grasps him by the coat sleeve and claims her dog, all dirty and disgraced as he is.

"I am very grateful, indeed," stammered Ella, as she held out her hand with some money toward the stranger, but he took no notice of her action, and lifting his apology for a hat, with a bow which would have done honor to a Chesterfield, was soon out of sight.

That identical tramp, for such he proved to be, called at Mrs. Winter's cottage a few days later, and Ella recognized her casual acquaintance, and in truth he looked the typical tramp—from his shirt-button, conspicuous by its absence, to his dusty shoes.

Mrs. Winter's pet aversion was a tramp; the very name suggested fire, and robbery, and murder; every rag and tatter had a terror for her, and when, perchance, she did give employment to such people, it was under the pressure of stern necessity, and always with fear and trepidation.

An anxious and hurried consultation with Jane in the kitchen disclosed the fact that the split kindling was exhausted, and upon the assurance of that intrepid person that she would "keep an eye on him," she was permitted to lead him to the wood-pile.

After sitting him down to dinner in the kitchen, Jane, acting upon pre-arrangement, took the liberty of giving Mrs. Winter "a wink," whereupon that wise and worthy woman ensconced herself behind a convenient ambush, and proceeded to study Mr. Tramp.

For the first time in her life the good woman's opinion wavered. The hat which nearly concealed his face when she first saw him, was now laid aside, disclosing to view a broad, white forehead, surmounted by a handsome crop of brown curls; his face was not over clean, but there was no mistaking the beauty in every line of it; a very youthful face, with not even the shadow of a mustache to hide the clear-cut, refined mouth. Truly, she " came and saw, and was conquered." The kind, motherly heart even felt a gentle thrill of pity for this poor boy, whose face, strangely enough, brought the memory of a dear dead boy back to her as she gazed.

" I will find some work for him," she said to herself.

She thought also of the flower garden, which needed looking after, and resolved to give him work for a few weeks.

They were soon busy among the weeds and flowers, Ella, and even Mrs. Winter taking a hand. The tramp proved himself a valuable acquisition. He preserved a stolid silence unless when spoken to. He never recalled the incident of the dog-fight, and looked blankly at Ella, as if he had never before seen her.

Ella thought there was something interesting in this slender, brown-eyed youth, who so badly played the *role* of tramp.

Owing to her secluded life, Ella Winter's ideas of men and things had been mostly gathered through the doubtful medium of the modern novel, therefore, she cannot be blamed if her romantic and highly imaginative mind found food and ample exercise in the daily study of this man, who was a perplexing mixture of gentleman and vagabond. They actually found it difficult to address him as an inferior, his manner leaving them in doubt as to his social standing among them, and Mrs. Winter had evidently divested herself of all her old prejudice and fears concerning tramps generally.

"What do you think of our gardener now, mamma?" inquired Ella one morning over her teacup.

"Oh, I think he's just splendid," answered her mother, looking radiantly at Ella through her glasses.

"What do you think I found him doing yesterday?" went on Ella.

Mrs. Winter looked up now and a shade of alarm crossed her face. Was she mistaken, after all? Was this fellow— but her fears were allayed by the smile upon Ella's face. "I surprised him reading *this*," said Ella, triumphantly holding up a small edition of "Les Miserables" in French.

"Oh, you should see him blush, mamma, and I think he was angry, too, for when I apologized, and told him to continue reading, would you believe it, he hardly thanked me."

The momentary doubt which crossed Mrs. Winter's mind, brought a little qualm of conscience with it. Did she do right, she questioned herself, in allowing her fears to be allayed by the fair face of the vagrant, who might be a thief or murderer in disguise?

The toast is drying up and the muffins are growing cold, but neither of these ladies seem to have any appetite this morning. Mrs. Winter's thoughts reverted to Willie Gaynor, and an earnest wish formed itself in her mind that he would come very soon.

Ella is helping the tramp to tie up some rose trees to-day, and drawing him into conversation, he astonishes her by his knowledge of books and their authors. His face lights up with enthusiasm, completely transforming the man. He speaks with rare judgment, and evinces undoubted taste and culture, but he soon checks himself as if by an effort, and assumes again his servile and almost sullen manner. He is more than ever an enigma to her. A few hours later he presented her with an exquisite half-blown rose, and *she* accepted it from this handsome tramp with as much grace and thanks as if it had been given her by a prince, aye, and blushed—to her chagrin—under his gaze, as she pinned it in her bosom.

There is not a word spoken about Willie Gaynor now, although he is expected in another week, and Ella wonders even to herself why she so seldom thinks of him. She has certainly lost much of the fervor with which she regarded his coming a month ago. She is afraid to question her heart, which could tell her a strange story from which she would almost recoil, could it give voice to the truth. For all troubles Ella invariably found a panacea in a chase with her beloved dogs. Calling "Nigger and Ruby," she held up a dainty forefinger, and then admonished them: "Nigger, if you quarrel with any of your relatives to-day, you shall never, *never* come out with me again." The dogs winked in an apologetic way, and wagged their tails in a manner suggestive of compliance. Tying her ample sun-hat under her chin, and putting tramps, troubles and cousin out of her mind, for the time, she set out for her beloved chase.

Meanwhile Mrs. Winter is holding an anxious and confidential confab with Jane in the pantry. She questions her closely concerning the movements, demeanor and possible designs of the still-to-be-feared tramp, to all of which Jane gives the most favorable answers, more-over, winding up with an emphatic assurance of his being, to her mind, "a perfect gentleman, never asks a question, and always speaks to her (Jane) as if she were a born lady." The warmth and enthusiasm of the girl's defense showed plainly enough that he had captured that side of the citadel, but she is still in doubt and uncertainty, and is glad that the time of Willie Gaynor's arrival is near at hand.

Ella finds herself a long distance from home; her nerves are at their highest tension to-day, and excitement renders her oblivious of time. The lengthening shadows warn her that it is growing late. Nigger and Ruby begin to look up appealingly to their young mistress, who, as yet, shows no sign of returning. She is walking now down a steep and rugged decline, an old water-course, whose rough stones, and fragments of rock make it extremely hazardous. She is thinking deeply, and takes little heed of her sur-roundings. Stepping upon a stone which looks firmly imbedded in the ground, it turns treacherously; she bal-ances upon it for a moment, then falls forward heavily. She attempts to rise, but to her dismay finds that her ankle is sprained, and sinks down with a cry of pain. There was little prospect of help in that desolate place. She wondered despairingly, what would become of her. In her extremity, she clung to Nigger, who whined piteously in sympathy with her. It was quite dark now. Nigger, real-izing the hopelessness of the situation, set up a dismal and prolonged howl, which was, had he but known it, the most effectual mode of assistance he could have rendered, for it fortunately reached the ear of a solitary wanderer, who was about to betake himself to his quarters for the night. He stood still for a moment and listened; again the melancholy cry was wafted on the night breeze, this time more distinctly. He set out quickly in the direction of the sound, and in a short time was beside our unlucky heroine. She looked up with great tearful eyes, full of thankfulness, to behold the "tramp."

"Oh! I'm so glad," she began brokenly, "I think I should have died here, if you had not come."

"And I'm so sorry that you have hurt yourself," he answered, with tender compassion in his voice. Presently he kneels down, and lifts her from her painful position. There is a softness in his touch, and a womanly tenderness in his movements, that fills her with a sense of rest and protection. She looked at him wonderingly, and can scarcely believe that he is the same person.

She is obliged to lean her head against him, and as it was a case of absolute necessity, no thought of compromising her dignity entered her head. Together they discuss the best means of getting home. She advises him to go to the cottage for the basket carriage, to which he agrees after some argument, but when he is ready, she positively refuses to be left alone, and finally agrees to be carried home in his arms.

If there is any one virtue in this mundane sphere of ours sufficient in itself to make a saint, it is the self-abnegation of the ordinary young man, who could bear such a precious burden for fully two miles, and not tighten his hold just the smallest perceptible bit. Whether Ella took this fact into consideration or not, no one can tell; but certain it is, that when he laid her tenderly and almost reverently upon her mother's lounge later on, she thanked him with a look in her eyes that spoke as plainly as words, her deep respect for him.

Willie Gaynor is coming to-morrow. Ella is confined to her bed. Mrs. Winter is worried and anxious. Jane announces later on that the "hired man" has not put in an appearance to-day, but at the same time, assures them that everything is in the "best of order." Mrs. Winter draws a sigh of relief, and Ella says nothing. She is actually cross to-day. There are times when even the most amiable girls are out of sorts. No one suggests a fresh flower, and there seems but little gladness in the house, somehow. Next day they carry Ella down to the parlor, and prop her around comfortably with pillows. Her golden-brown hair is lying loosely, forming a pretty framework to her face.

At five o'clock there is a grinding of wheels on the gravel outside, and a minute later Mrs. Winter is holding out both hands to a tall, grey-haired man—Willie's father. After the congratulations were over Mr. Gaynor looked around as if he expected to see someone else, and, at last, to everyone's astonishment, asked where Willie was.

"Just what I was going to ask you," replied Mrs. Winter.

"I suppose the young rascal is not willing to go home yet," continued Mr. Gaynor, with a sly glance at Ella, and not seeming to notice Mrs. Winter's remark. Ella returns his glance with one of blank bewilderment, and while they are all looking askance at each other the door-bell gets a peremptory tug, which nearly starts them all to their feet.

"That's his ring," said Mr. Gaynor; "he always turns it into an alarm." Jane opens the door promptly enough, but afterwards stands rooted to the ground in astonishment, as "the tramp" stalks past her and goes *sans ceremonie* straight towards the parlor. She retreated to the kitchen in a sort of stupor, which took away the power of thought. The worthy woman sinks helplessly into a chair. Meanwhile the cause of her perplexity is endeavoring to explain how his love of adventure induced him to adopt the *role* of tramp, and looks as contrite as the laugh in his mischievous brown eyes will permit.

"I should have cautioned you, Margaret," said Mr. Gaynor, trying to look severe. "I might have known he would do something of the kind. You young rascal!" he continued, trying to concentrate a ferocious glare through his spectacles upon the culprit. "Even his own father is not safe from his pranks."

Mrs. Winter protests valiantly that she knew him all the time, and as for Ella, she flashes one reproachful look at him, and then hides a very crimson face among the pillows.

"And by way of punishment you shall march home with me to-morrow," said Mr. Gaynor. "I'm certain these ladies won't think of tolerating you any longer."

Willie Gaynor is stooping over his cousin and tries to read her face, which is a difficult task, owing to the different feelings which have been depicted thereon for the last half hour. Her heart, which has been eddying round in a whirl of distress for the last month, is settling down and a sense of rest, and peace and certainty is stealing upon her, but a little throb of revenge alone mars the present still. She makes a silent and secret vow to have satisfaction, in some way, for this joke, of which she has clearly been the victim.

"He shall never, *never* know that I cared for him. He shall never say that I fell in love with a 'tramp.'" And her face crimsoned at her own thoughts.

"*You* will not send me away," said he in a low voice, and he tries to take her hand. "I claim pardon on the

score of at least *one* good service. What would have
become of you if I had not been playing my *role* the night
of your accident? Even 'tramps' can be useful sometimes," he said.

Her anger is fading, dying miserably; the tell-tale color
comes and goes beneath his glance, making her face an
open page.

"Shall I go home with father, to-morrow?" he inquired-
softly.

"You ought to," she replied petulantly, making a last
desperate effort to appear unconcerned. "You have lost
a whole month for nothing, and scared us almost to death
into the bargain."

"A whole month lost," he answered musingly, not seeming to notice her last sentence.

The belligerent blood came into her cheeks again, as
she half defined his meaning,

"What will people think?" she resumed, not deigning
to notice the hint conveyed in his last words. "What will
Jane say?" Here a faint smile betrayed itself in the cor-
ners of her mouth, as the intense ludicrousness of the situation became more apparent.

Willie Gaynor is making an effort to assume a contrite
expression, but at this juncture he laughs outright.

"As for Jane, I think," he says, "I have a stout ally in
her, and am certain that *she*, at least, will have none the
less welcome for me."

There is little more to be said. The mischief-loving,
prank-playing tramp, had so far won his way to all hearts
at the cottage, that he did not leave it until he carried off
the owner of the most rebellious, but withal the most
lovable one.

A Sweet Singer.

I am a passionate lover of music, and never miss an opportunity of gratifying my desires in that respect. A woman's voice in song, has for me, a peculiar and powerful charm. Under its influence I am swayed, entranced; my faculties become enthralled until I am oblivious to surroundings, forgetful of past and present.

Going to hear a debutante fills me with the most delicious anticipation. My friend, the young Prince de N——, had asked me to accompany him to hear a young English artist of whom great things had been promised.

"They say the English cantatrice has a lovely face also," observed the prince that evening, as we sat over our coffee, "a lovely face and a sweet voice," he murmured more to himself than to me, as he leaned back in his chair, and gazed through the heavy fringes of his half-closed eyes at the chandelier.

This Italian was a handsome fellow, with the face and form of an Apollo, fascinating beyond description, bright, debonnaire, and gay——alas, too gay, for his pleasures were often obtained at a heavy cost, and an utter disregard of consequences. Actresses, young and pretty, were his especial prey, and as I watched his face that night, I sighed involuntarily for the web of danger which was certainly being woven for one more woman.

We were early at the Port Saint Martine. The prince's

box, close to the stage, was a marvel of silver and velvet and glass mirrors multiplied you from all sides, affording ample and elegant views of back, front and profile.

The curtain had not yet been raised. I occupied the spare time in studying the prince, which was an easy task, as his face was at all times like an open book; he never took the trouble to mask his feelings, good or bad. He spoke but little to-night, and kept his eyes continually upon the stage. It was the opera of "La Sonnambula." "Amina" was the part chosen by the young debutante, who came upon the stage with nervous footsteps, looking very white and tremulous. I felt a pleasurable disappointment. The sweet cameo-like face was quite guiltless of what is known in stage parlance as "make up," the youthful, almost childish figure was clothed in an inartistic, almost clumsy manner, suggesting nothing of the actress, but a great deal of what was pure and womanly.

I fancied I could hear a murmur of disappointment from the vast crowd. The effect upon the generality of theatre-goers was not a pleasing one. Most people expect to see—even in a debutante—the "chic" and stagy style to which they are accustomed. But the fancied murmur soon died out and the great audience held an expectant breath. She commenced to sing; tremulously came the notes at first, her lips, like a cupid's bow, trembled pitifully for a moment or two, then the wavering words grew sweet and strong, soaring upwards as if the music bore them on its wings, sowing the air, as it were, with wondrous melody.

What an awakener of sweet and sad memories is a sympathetic voice! Truly there are depths within our hearts unsounded, good lying deep and dormant, to which only good music, pleading and passionate, can reach.

The pallid, lily-like face was transformed now, life and

light shone from it, faintly at first, then came radiant color to the cheeks, and the large, lustrous eyes seemed to emit light from their lovely depths.

She sang as if her very soul went out with her song; the frail figure swayed in the ecstasy of emotion; she looked and must have felt, like a goddess of music, ready to immolate herself upon the altar of her God.

"Dios!" exclaimed the prince, whom I had forgotten, and who, I have no doubt, was oblivious of my existence.

"What a voice," I replied.

Without seeming to hear me, he murmured, "What a face."

There must have been a serpent-like fascination about his expression just then, because I tried to turn my eyes to the stage, but they seemed riveted upon him.

While my gaze was still upon his face, Amina had been discovered in the Count's chamber. Her pathetic protestations of innocence, simple, child-like, though powerful, crept into callous hearts, and moistened eyes that had seldom known a tear. I am a man of the world, sinful, mayhap, but never can I forget the feeling of pure love and charity which that woman's voice created in my hardened heart. She felt the part, and made others feel for her; you knew she was a wronged and wretched woman, sobbing out her suffering heart.

Women cried audibly, and men were busy with their handkerchiefs; by an effort I took my eyes from the stage, and turned them upon the prince. Heaven! what a change was there. I scarcely recognized my friend of fifteen years. Amazement was so visible upon my face that he must have seen it, for he looked uneasily at me and turned away. His face was haggard and old, great drops of perspiration stood out upon his forehead, and a strange light, which I had never seen before, was in his eyes. His thoughts were evidently far away, for I spoke to him and he never heard me.

I felt alarmed, and shook him by the arm. He came to himself with an effort, and grasped my hand in seeming gratitude, then he put the other hand to his forehead with an air of weariness and begged me to accompany him home.

The opera was not yet over, but he did not seem to care. I looked once more at Amina, and involuntarily closed my eyes so they could retain the last glimpse of her.

That the prince had undergone some great mental change, was apparent. What memories of remorse that singer's face and voice might have brought vividly back to him, even I, his bosom friend, never knew.

I lost sight of him for many days; at length he sought me. He was very pale and quiet, with traces of suffering on his handsome face.

" Pierre, I am going to see the English Madamoiselle," he said, " Will you come with me?"

I replied, " Certainly."

Would I be ready in an hour? Yes. I thought of many things within that hour. Times were when this man would have been in the " green room " the very first night, and it was a rare case, indeed, when the prima donna's name was not linked with his through the mud and mire of Paris next day. I dreaded nothing of the kind now, and yet I could wish that he might not meet her.

We were soon at Miss R——'s hotel, sent up our cards, and found ourselves confronted by the manager a suave and smiling little Frenchman, who declared himself " heartbroken because he could not induce the beautiful English madamoiselle to be honored by an interview with us." In words which were honied over, as it were, he vaguely intimated " that slanderous tongues (no doubt) had linked our illustrious names, with deeds which he would be a monster to credit, but alas! you know, messieurs, how easily a woman believes," and with a heavenly smile which was beautifully tinged with a becoming shade of sorrow, he bowed us out.

The prince was miserable and I had a fellow feeling for him. We watched her day by day, walking and riding in the parks; he was never absent from his post, and my pity for him grew stronger, for I knew that my love for her was but a shadow compared with his. Yes, I dared to love her that first night, and yet, if I could, I would not touch the hem of her garment.

I began to fear for the prince's reason and made the most extraordinary efforts to get him introduced, but all to no purpose.

Things went on in this way till at length he rushed into my room one day; his eyes flashed with some of their old brilliancy, and his cheeks were flushed with excitement.

"I have it at last," exclaimed he. " Oh, my good friend, you will help me, you must help me."

I grasped him—he was weak as a child—and made him sit down. He held on to my hand and looked up beseechingly.

"I can sing, Pierre," he continued, " I used to sing well—I can do so again. They want a tenor—I will present myself—I will disguise—they will never know me. Pierre, don't stop me," he begged, seeing signs of disapproval in my face. "I shall and must."

I promised to help him and he grew calm, then going to the piano he commenced to play snatches of opera, then he drifted into the old ballads of the "Vandeville."

He had an exquisite voice, and yet I had never heard him sing.

He made his application and strangely enough was accepted. When he came to me again I scarcely knew him. He was minus the handsomest mustache in Paris, but a whole sun of happiness shone from his face.

"I have seen her, oh, Pierre, and she has heard me sing, and praised me." He would be with her, near her, and that was heaven enough for him.

Oh, love, what a powerful factor thou art for good or for evil! After he left me, a miserable pang of jealousy made a contemptible wretch of me, but I fought against it. The little good in me asserted itself and I was soon able to rejoice in my friend's joy.

He traveled and sang with her for two years. "This woman," he wrote to me, "has taught me how to live—how to love. She is a bright light upon my path without which I must have forever groped amidst the dead sea fruit of a misspent life.

Eventually he won his way to the heart of the prima donna, who never knew that she was marrying the Prince de N—— until the eve of her nuptials in London, when I had the happiness to be present.

A Broken Heart.

Down in the heart of Kent, that most beautiful of English counties stands the grand old Norman castle of Avonleigh. Built upon a gentle elevation, it commands a splendid view of the richest scenery, broad stretches of forest, whose giant trees dwindle into mere atoms in the distance, gently undulating hills, merging into the bluest skies, with here and there a tiny glimpse of silver sea.

It was the eve of that most disastrous internal struggle "The War of the Roses," when the fair flag of England was stained with the blood of her noblest sons. Lord John de Grey, the master of Avonleigh, had already declared himself a warm adherent of the house of York, and when the tide of war mingled its turbulent stream with the pure and peaceful waters of domestic life, the grey-haired earl was found fighting bravely beside his only son.

A mellow day in autumn is drawing to a close; the soft light of a harvest moon is contending for supremacy with the shadows of a sinking sun. In a little while the castle is bathed in the tender moonlight, the clinging ivy leaves glisten like silver and tremble from the faintest perfumed breeze.

The earl's only daughter, Lady Miriam, a fair-haired maiden, with a wondrously beautiful face, is down in the quaint old garden, drawn thither by the singular beauty of the night; and, verily, moon never shone upon fairer form

8

than hers, and the flowers sent forth their sleeping incense to greet this living " Rose of Avonleigh."

As she stoops to pluck a white rose from its thorny stem, the delicate finger was pierced and a crimson drop stained the rose's purity, but no murmur escaped her, and gathering up the folds of her white robe, she walked slowly back to the castle.

Young and beautiful, surrounded with wealth and pleasures, this young girl knew not what unhappiness meant; like a bird whose gilded cage protects and shelters her, life, indeed, was all sunshine without a shadow.

Though rumors of war were in the air, and men spoke in serious tones of the strife which seemed inevitable, no thought of danger marred the calm happiness of her existence.

Already she had given her heart to young Wilfred Aylmer, as brave and handsome a youth as the sun ever shone upon, and whose strong young arm shall also be wielded in the cause of the noble house of York.

Through the wide, dimly-lighted hallway Lady Miriam walked slowly and almost unconsciously, clasping the now half-crimsoned rose to her bosom, until she reached her father's study.

The old earl sat in profound thought, and did not heed the soft footfall until a tender cheek was laid against his own.

"What a dark, brown study my dear father is in," murmured the sweet voice.

The earl's face was seamed and shadowed with care as he lifted his head, and a sudden paleness overspread his features when he saw the white rose which she laughingly held up to his gaze.

"I was thinking of you, my pearl," he replied, drawing

the fair head down to him, and kissing the sweet, childish
mouth, "but now that you are here," he added, "like a
gleam of sunlight among my shadows, I am no longer
sad." But seeing a shade of pain in her eyes, he added
hastily:

"I was indeed thinking of the time when someone would
rob me of the fairest flower in my garden of roses."

She chided him lovingly for "thinking too soon," and with
her accustomed prayer and good-night kiss, left him.

Up the wide staircase she goes, slowly and thoughtfully,
now through the great picture gallery, where the old-
fashioned but beautiful faces of other Lady Miriams looked
down upon her. Was it the weird moonlight that made
those dead faces seem to bend from their stiff frames and
cause a gleam of sadness to light the dead eyes that seemed
to follow her as she passed beneath them?

She soon reached her favorite room, high in the west
wing, a cozy nook, where she loved to look upon the moonlight scene without, and inhale the faint fragrance of the
garden beneath.

Lady Miriam's life had indeed been like to the unruffled
bosom of a clear, calm lake. Her placid bosom had never
been disturbed by a sad thought. True, within the past
few months her heart had awakened, bud-like, to the new
and sweet knowledge of another love. That very morning
she had been plighted to Sir Wilfred Aylmer, and their
marriage would be solemnized when this war-cloud had
rolled past.

Long and sadly the earl mused that night; his heart was
full of foreboding of coming sorrow. What if in this war,
which every day seemed more imminent, he should fall?
What if this, his one ewe lamb, should be orphaned—
desolate? He tried to drive away his gloomy imaginings

by recalling the sweet face of her who had just left him with words of love and hope, and prayed that this " bitter chalice" might pass away.

But, alas! a month later saw the rival parties engaged in determined and deadly strife—saw also the white-haired earl and his son fighting side by side with young Wilfred Aylmer.

Oh, selfish kings and avaricious princes, how little ye reck the cost of your crowns!—how little ye care! News traveled slowly in those days, but mediæval maidens did not sigh and pine like us of modern times, but looked hopefully for the triumphant return of their victors, their minds being molded and tinted by their warlike surroundings. Battles boded only an access of honor and glory.

Rumors at length reached Avonleigh that a great and decisive battle had been fought, in which the house of York had triumphed. Preparations on a magnificent scale had commenced at the castle for the return of the victors. Joy bells rang from every steeple and belfry in the village. All were jubilant in the belief that their noble lord was coming home covered with honors. Ah, but here was a messenger at last riding in hot haste, who looked neither to the right nor the left as he rode past the gay banners and the resounding cheers of the happy villagers. Both horse and man were sore, jaded, and covered with foam from long and continued riding, but he never drew rein until he reached the castle, whose gates are thrown wide open, bar and bolt giving way to graceful arches and emblems of welcome.

In the outer courtyard he flings the reins to a servant, who stares at him in silent wonder. Another astonished lackey is requested to lead him to the presence of the Lady Miriam.

Through gorgeously decorated halls, where the air is heavy with the odor of flowers, huge vases of white roses greet the eye at every step, dropping, as if in welcome, their rich petals at his feet. Truly the fairest and fittest welcome to the victor.

Geoffry Vane was a brave gentleman and a gallant soldier, who had often confronted death in many shapes— a man to whom fear was a word without meaning—yet to-day his heart sank weakly and his limbs trembled as the rustle of a woman's dress fell upon his ears. In another moment he is bending low before Miriam Grey, who is his cousin, and whom he has never seen until to-day.

There is a glad and gracious welcome in her face and her voice as she holds out her hands to him. Ah! how can he tell her the story which may quench the light in those bright eyes forever, or mayhap chill to death the white hand now lying in his own!

Oh, victorious white rose, whose beauty is sullied by the life-blood of father, lover, and brother, well may you droop your heads in the great halls below, and shed your pale leaves in pity for her whose peerless head is well-nigh leveled with the dust. Aye, this day of glorious victory brings grief unutterable to the now desolate Lady Miriam.

**

The red October winds are sighing among the gables and turrets of the castle, whispering the woeful tale to the leafless trees and dead flowers. The crimson and gold leaves are being buried beneath the snow which is piling high above them, and all nature puts on her saddest garb as the magnificent mausoleum at Avonleigh closes its ponderous doors upon the dead victors.

Like a white shadow the hapless Lady Miriam paces ever through the lonely halls and galleries, where the dead

roses are still untouched.   No hand has been allowed to
remove the withered emblems of welcome since that fatal
day.

Frozen and cold as the beauteous eidelweiss she has
buried herself from the world.   Patiently and hopelessly
has Geoffry Vane tried to warm the dead heart to life.
Long and tenderly he has hoped that the stricken heart-
tendrils might revive and bloom again in the sunshine of
his love.

The spring-time has come again with its soft blue skies.
The tender flower buds are unfolding to the sun-god,
whose breath nurses them from the brown bosom of the
earth.   The summer has come with all its gladness, but
yet no bloom comes to the cheeks of the widowed girl—
no brightness to the sad eyes.

Again the October moon is bathing the castle of Avonleigh in its yellow light, flinging grotesque shadows upon the
stately mausoleum, and the dying flowers are sending forth
their last perfumed sigh ere the rude touch of winter comes
upon them.   Up in her boudoir the golden head is bowed
in prayer; she hears not a footstep until Geoffry Vane
utters her name reverently.   She lifts her head, looking
at him with eyes which seem to emit the very light of
heaven itself.   His heart bounds with a great joy.   At
last she is awaking to his patient love.   The cold hands
are not withdrawn from his now.   For the first time the
weary head is resting against his heart.   At last his unwearied
love has found an echo in the sweet bosom and moistened
the parched heart.   The lips which his warm kisses fall
upon for the first time are cold, but oh, the love and life

and promise that he sees in the ineffable smile with which she tries to reward him! It was truly

> A moment's gleam of sun,
>   Sweetening the very edge of doom;
> The past, the present—all that fate
> Can bring of dark or desperate
>   Around such hours,
> But make them cast
> Intenser radiance while they last.

Speechless with his great happiness he holds her closely in his arms. For one brief moment the beautiful lips are upraised to his, and in that one long kiss the wounded white rose breathes her last loving sigh, and Geoffry Vane holds the dead Lady Miriam in his close embrace.